I0630240

Holiday Loss

JANE BLYTHE

Copyright © 2023 by Jane Blythe

All rights reserved.

No part of this book may be reproduced in any form or by any electronic or mechanical means, including information storage and retrieval systems, without written permission from the author, except for the use of brief quotations in a book review.

Cover designed by Q Designs

❀ Created with Vellum

Acknowledgments

I'd like to thank everyone who played a part in bringing this story to life. Particularly my mom who is always there to share her thoughts and opinions with me. My wonderful cover designer Amy who did an amazing job with this stunning cover. My fabulous editor Lisa for all the hard work she puts into polishing my work. My awesome team, Sophie, Robyn, and Clayr, without your help I'd never be able to run my street team. And my fantastic street team members who help share my books with every share, comment, and like!

And of course a big thank you to all of you, my readers! Without you I wouldn't be living my dreams of sharing the stories in my head with the world!

CHAPTER

One

December 1st
11:12 P.M.

"Break in in progress at one one four Lennox Road."

Detective Jessica Spears startled as the dispatcher's voice echoed through her otherwise quiet car. The address took a moment to register, but once it did, she realized it was her favorite restaurant. Most people in the town's favorite restaurant.

Eat Dessert First was a family-friendly place with an obvious motto that she'd taken her seven-year-old son to dozens of times. There was also a quieter, more romantic area toward the back where couples often went for dates. Not that she even remembered what going on a date was like it had been so long. Being a single mom and a cop didn't leave much time for anything else.

Since she was only two blocks away from the restaurant, she quickly called in that she would check it out even though she'd already clocked out for the day and was supposed to be heading home to relieve the babysitter.

As much as she couldn't wait to sneak into her little boy's room and give him a goodnight kiss even though she'd missed out on tucking him in, there was no way she wasn't going to follow up on the call. The restaurant was run by a sweet older woman who was adored by everyone in town. While she didn't know Mrs. Grayson personally, she knew the woman had been a struggling single mom before being swept up into a modern-day fairytale when she'd wound up marrying her billionaire boss. Instead of deciding to live the rest of her life in luxury, she'd made her dreams come true and opened up a restaurant that was still going strong two decades later.

Jessica admired the woman for creating such an amazing place that managed to appeal to every single demographic and made it work so that couples wanting a romantic night out didn't feel put off by the family dinners and giggling children. The food was amazing, hitting all the comfort zones, and the desserts were out of this world.

Turning the corner and heading for the restaurant, she took a moment to wonder what she'd ever do if she met a billionaire. Only ...

The idea was so preposterous that she couldn't even come up with an answer.

Where would she meet a billionaire?

At the precinct where she worked?

At the grocery store?

At one of her son's soccer games?

She didn't even get to go to those as often as she'd like because she was working so many hours just to keep a roof over their heads and food on the table.

Ever since her partner Adam Abram married Jasmine, she'd tried to impose as little as possible to give the family more time together. Both she and Adam had been single parents, his daughter Claire just a year younger than Freddie. While they'd both been single, they'd had a system where they helped each other out, and while she knew that Adam would still be more than happy to keep helping, she felt like she was intruding now that he had a new wife.

Not that she thought Jasmine wouldn't want to help either, the woman was sweet and always happy to babysit, but they were a family now and she wanted them to enjoy that time together without her son hanging around.

Which meant more of her paycheck went on sitters than it ever had in the past.

There was no family to help her out. When her husband had decided that married life was not for him, he'd divorced her and left her to raise their then two-year-old son alone. According to her parents that was her fault. If she'd been a better wife, given up her job, pampered her husband like they believed he deserved then he wouldn't have left.

If the man was so wonderful, why didn't he pay child support?

He'd just left. Left her with a toddler, no support, a house she couldn't afford, and a struggle that would last at least until her son turned eighteen.

As she pulled up outside the restaurant and thought of all the good times she'd shared there with her little boy, Jessica knew she'd do it all over again, working just as hard, harder even, whatever it took, because those moments with her son made all the exhaustion and stress more than worth it.

There was no sign of anyone at the front door, so she slipped out of her car and headed for the back of the building. Assuming she was going to find some kids thinking the restaurant was an easy target, her hand hovered near her weapon, but she hadn't pulled it out yet.

First, she'd assess the situation and then decide how to proceed.

Rounding the corner, she immediately spotted the would-be thief.

They were standing by the door, from the looks of things attempting to pick the lock, only they must be doing a pretty poor job of it given they were still out there and had been long enough to be spotted, for it to be called in, and for her to arrive.

Amateur.

Which made her job easier.

Since there was only one perpetrator, Jessica kept her hand near her weapon but again didn't pull it out.

"Sir, please step away from the door and put your hands where I can see them," she ordered as she walked toward the man in black.

The figure startled and went to turn, putting her on alert.

When she walked into her job each day she had only one goal.

Make it home to her son alive.

Freddie already had a dad who didn't want him and wouldn't support him, he wasn't going to lose his mom as well.

"Sir, don't turn around, hands in the air," she ordered, pulling her weapon free. Better to be safe than sorry. For all she knew this was a junkie high on drugs who could be dangerous and unpredictable. Or it could be some silly kid trying to impress his friends. Or it could be a member of a gang. There were too many options not to be cautious.

"If I could just explain—"

"No, you can't," she said, close enough now that she could reach out and snap a handcuff around one of the man's wrists. There would be no explanations until she knew she was safe and had this man under control.

Only when she had both of his wrists secured behind his back did she turn him and see the most incredible pair of gray eyes staring down at her, dancing with amusement.

Amusement?

That sparked anger in her.

Not only had he prevented her from already being home with her little boy to grab a few hours of sleep before she had to get up and do it all over again, but he thought this was funny.

Let's see how funny he thought it was after spending the night in a jail cell.

"Sir, you're under arrest for attempted breaking and entering," she announced with satisfaction.

"You're making a mistake," he informed her.

"That's what they all say."

CHAPTER

Two

December 1st
    11:19 P.M.

While he could tell the pretty cop disagreed, Donovan Davidson found this whole thing highly amusing.

If she'd just given him a second to explain, she would have known there was no need to cuff him and haul him over to her car. She'd shoved him in the backseat with an air of exhaustion, and he was overcome by a need to do something to fix that.

Fixing things was what he was good at. Or at least it was when it came to money. With women? Not so much.

"A unit is coming to take you into the precinct," the woman informed him.

"You going to give me a chance to explain myself now, beautiful?" he asked.

Anger flared in the prettiest pair of green eyes he'd ever had the pleasure of staring into, and red stained her cheeks.

True as the compliment was, Donovan immediately regretted it. His mother had raised him to be more respectful than that to both women, and law enforcement. Once he asked the pretty cop out on a date and she said yes *then* he could call her beautiful all he wanted, but not now.

"I'm sorry, that was out of line," he said before she could tell him off. "True, but out of line. I wasn't breaking in there to steal anything tonight. This is my mother's restaurant. I'm Donovan Davidson, Sylvia Grayson's son. My mom left her keys in there tonight and didn't realize until she got home. I was visiting and didn't want her coming out this late on her own, so I said I'd come and get them for her. Unfortunately, my lock-picking skills weren't up to the job. It's harder than it looks," he joked.

Those green eyes narrowed, and she was clearly trying to figure out if he was telling her the truth. Probably didn't help that he looked nothing like his mom. Only his little sister had gotten her fair, almost pixie-like features. Both he and his two older brothers took after the father who had walked out on them all leaving their mom to struggle with five mouths to feed. It was no wonder all four of them were protective of her even if it had been a little over two decades since she married their stepfather, a billionaire who had given her the life she deserved and worshipped the ground she walked on.

"We can call her," he added. "She'll corroborate everything I just said."

Before the woman could respond, a car screeched into the parking lot. Not a cop car, his stepfather's car. And that right there was why he approved of the man for his mom, because he'd insisted on driving her despite the late hour. The cops had probably called his mom to let her know someone was trying to break into her restaurant, and she'd come roaring down there to make sure he was okay. She wouldn't have been able to call him because he'd purposefully left his phone at her place, not wanting to be bothered if he got another call from his stalker.

"Actually, we can do better than call. I think that's her there," Donovan said, nodding to the car that two people were hurrying out of.

"Mrs. Grayson?" the cop asked.

"Yes. What's going on? Why is my son in the back of a police car?" Mom demanded. Despite her tiny size, she could be an intimidating figure when she had to be. Usually, she was soft-spoken and jovial, like a tiny little Santa Claus. But mess with one of her kids and her mama bear came out in full force.

"A misunderstanding, ma'am," the cop replied. "There was a report of someone trying to break into your restaurant. When I got here he was picking the lock."

"I left my keys inside, he was just trying to get them," Mom explained.

"Yes, I'm aware of that now," the cop said with a weary sigh. "Turn around, sir, and I'll remove the cuffs."

"Handcuffs?" Mom squeaked in that tone that said she was close to letting loose and giving the cop a piece of her mind. Undeserved. The woman hadn't known who he was and was just doing her job.

Luckily, his stepfather agreed. "Procedure I'm sure, darling," he said, wrapping an arm around his wife's shoulders and tucking her against his side.

"She could have let him explain before treating him like a common criminal," Mom huffed.

"You're right, I should have let him explain," the woman said as she unsnapped the handcuffs and stepped back to let him out. "I'm sorry for the misunderstanding, of course you are free to go. Do you need help getting into the building to retrieve your keys, ma'am?"

"Actually, we were able to find the spare set," Mom replied. "Let's get you home, baby boy," she fussed, looping an arm around his and trying to guide him toward where she must have spotted his car. Not fazed by her babying him, it was just her way, he gently tugged his arm free.

"Something I have to do before I go," he told her. "I'll see you at your place in a bit."

Hurrying over to the pretty cop's car, he caught her just as she was climbing into the driver's seat. There was something about this woman that called out to him. Even as hard as the first eight years of his life had been, Donovan believed in fate, fairytales, true love, and soul mates. He had to. He'd seen it firsthand.

"No hard feelings about tonight," he said, grabbing the door before she could close it.

"Thank you. I'm sorry I didn't listen." Again, there was weariness in her voice, and again he felt a powerful need to help in some way. To fix things for her even though he wasn't sure what exactly it was that needed fixing.

"It's fine, I'm sure you've heard it all before," he assured, shooting her what he thought was his most charming smile.

"I have actually," she said, huffing a small chuckle. "You wouldn't believe some of the excuses I get told."

"I'm sure some of them are really creative. Can I take you out to dinner tomorrow night?" No point in beating around the bush. He was attracted to her and wanted to get to know her.

Surprise had her mouth dropping open. "I just put you in hand-cuffs. You don't even know my name."

"There's an easy fix for that."

A small smile transformed her face from pretty to breathtakingly stunning. "It's Jessica." The smile fell from her face. "But I'm sorry, Mr. Davidson, I don't have time for dating."

With that, she closed her door and started up her car.

Donovan stood there, watching as the taillights disappeared down the street. He'd been raised to respect women and knew no meant no. Only Jessica hadn't said she didn't want to go on a date with him, she'd said she didn't have time for dating.

A big difference.

One thing she was going to learn about him was that when he set his eyes on something, he worked hard until he got it.

CHAPTER
Three

December 2nd
8:34 A.M.

It felt like she'd never left.

Jessica swallowed a yawn as she tried to focus on the screen in front of her.

Sleep had remained elusive for most of the night. She'd felt bad about not giving Donovan Davidson a chance to explain himself, assuming he was doing what the call-in had accused him of, and embarrassed for being so wrong about things even if she was only doing her job and acting on the intel she had.

Then there were the dreams.

When sleep finally did come, her dreams were filled with a dark-haired man with gray eyes and a charming smile. For the first time in she couldn't even remember how long, she had dreamed about sex. Waking when the alarm went off with a throbbing between her legs and a heavy weight of unfulfilled need clinging to her.

As always, the morning rushed by in a whirl of trying to get herself and her seven-year-old ready for the day simultaneously, while also trying not to think about the fact that a man had asked her out on a date.

Five years had passed since she'd gotten divorced, and she hadn't been on a date since.

There was just no time.

Exactly what she said to Donovan last night when he asked if he could take her to dinner. Her experience said that most men were interested in having sex with her but not in taking on all the baggage she had being a single mom with an ex who contributed nothing toward his son's care.

Just because she hadn't been asked out on a date didn't mean she hadn't been propositioned. Usually, as soon as she told them she had a kid and dating her would have to fit around that they ran a mile.

A nice little ego boost, that was all last night could be. It was a nice compliment that a billionaire as she knew Mrs. Grayson's children to be would ask her out, especially given the awkwardness of her having cuffed and arrested him. Add in that Donovan was attractive, and yeah, it definitely felt nice even if there was no way she would have said yes.

As soon as he knew about her son, he would have taken those words back.

For now, she had to accept that dating wasn't in the cards. Work and Freddie were all she could handle on her plate right now. Maybe one day, when her son went off to college, she could think about re-entering the dating pool, scary though that would be.

So what if sometimes she was overcome with loneliness?

All things considered, she had a pretty good life. Her son was an amazing little human, she loved her job, she had great friends, and she was content knowing that even though her family had thrown her away when she got divorced, she would never do that to her child.

"Hey, Jess."

"Yeah?" Looking away from the computer screen, she rubbed at her bleary eyes. Not enough sleep was catching up with her. Maybe this weekend she'd have to convince Freddie to stay in, take things easy, watch movies, play video games, and wrap presents, ready to start following their holiday traditions and start delivering them soon.

"Someone had these delivered for you," Adam told her.

Blinking away the grittiness that seemed stuck in her eyes, her mouth dropped open in shock when she saw what her partner held.

It was the biggest bouquet she'd ever seen.

So big in fact that Adam could hardly hold it.

There were at least half a dozen different flowers and a myriad of colors. Pretty pinks and purples, brighter reds and yellows, all mixed in with the greenery to make it look like a rainbow had touched the ground and someone had gathered up the evidence and put it together.

Beautiful, no other word to describe it, but not for her.

Couldn't be.

Who would send her flowers?

"What do you mean they were delivered to me?" she asked, pushing away from her desk and standing up but not taking a step toward her partner or the flowers.

"Card has your name on it, and the driver had your name and this address," Adam said, his dark eyes sparkling with curiosity.

They were friends and their shared understanding of how hard it was to be a single parent had brought them even closer. They shared most things, and it was obvious her partner was wondering why she hadn't mentioned a boyfriend.

Only there was no boyfriend.

There wasn't even a boy.

Well, man not boy.

Other than friends, people related to work, or people related to Freddie's school, the only man she'd even conversed with lately was ...

No.

He wouldn't.

Would he?

"Something you want to tell me?" Adam asked as he set the giant bouquet down on her desk.

"Umm ... no. Nothing." Despite how it seemed that was absolutely the truth.

"Certainly seems like there should be. You seeing someone and failed to mention it?"

"Seeing someone? When would I even have the time?" Her hand trembled as it reached out to grasp the card sitting amongst the flowers.

"Then who's sending you flowers?"

"I don't know," she answered honestly. Just because she had a crazy idea of who it might be didn't mean it was true.

"One way to find out." Adam nodded at the card in her hand.

Slowly, she opened it, almost afraid to see who they were from. "If you feel like teaching me the ropes of lock picking the offer for dinner still stands," she read aloud, her voice shaking as much as her hands.

It was from him.

From Donovan Davidson.

"Lock picking? Someone asked you out and asked you to teach them how to pick locks?" Adam asked, clearly confused.

Embarrassed about last night, she hadn't told him about it this morning, hadn't thought there was any need to. Hadn't believed that a billionaire like Donovan would give her a second thought.

But he had.

More than that he'd sent her flowers.

After handcuffing him and putting him in the back of her car, he'd still asked her out. Even when she'd said no, he'd reached out again.

Why did that have excited butterflies dancing in her stomach when she knew it could never go anywhere?

CHAPTER
Four

December 6th
   5:44 P.M.

This out-of-character nervousness was exciting even as it was unpleasant.

Donovan was used to being confident. He knew his skills, his strengths and weaknesses, and plenty of people called him egotistical, but he never viewed it that way. It wasn't that he thought he was good at everything, he just focused on the things he could do instead of those he couldn't.

With the amount of money he had sitting in his portfolio of investments, properties, and stocks, combined with the body he spent hours a day working on at the gym, he had never had a shortage of women interested in getting him into bed. Over the years, he'd dated but not a single woman had captured his interest more than the exhausted cop who had put him in handcuffs.

Getting her out of his mind had been impossible the last three days.

Along with the flowers he'd been sending each morning to the precinct he'd included a card with his phone number. While Jessica had yet to call him, she also hadn't contacted him to tell him that she wanted him to stop sending flowers.

He was taking that as a win.

A small victory but still a win nonetheless.

Today he was bringing the flowers in person.

If she rejected him then he could handle it. Well, the ball of anxiety in his stomach told him he wouldn't like it, but he was a grown-up, and if she wasn't interested, then it was better he knew that now than down the track.

Following the directions he'd been given, he entered a large room and spotted her immediately. Her mane of dark red locks made her stand out in any room, and seeing her again, this time in the full light, she was even more stunning than he remembered.

Like some cosmic force was at work, her head lifted, turning in his direction. Her eyes widened when she spotted him standing there, the bouquet in his hands, but her gaze never wavered, locked on his like the universe was insisting they forge a connection.

That's what it felt like to him anyway.

The spell was only broken when a young boy's voice called out.

"Hey, Mom, can we bake brownies for dessert tonight?"

Startling, Jessica turned as a little boy with a mop of brown hair and a little blonde girl walked into the room along with a man.

All three of them headed toward Jessica.

For a moment the bottom dropped out of his world.

She was married?

With two kids?

Why wouldn't she tell him to back the hell off when he asked her out if she already had a family?

Her words from that night echoed in his mind. *I'm sorry, Mr. Davidson, I don't have time for dating.*

Didn't have time because she had a husband, a son, and a daughter at home.

Anger took hold and he was about to turn and head out when Jessica spoke to the man who had brought in the kids. "Tell Jasmine thank you for picking Freddie up from school for me last minute."

"It's no worry, she was happy to do it," the man replied. There was a huge smile on his face as he looked from Jessica to Donovan. "You need us to take Freddie for the night?"

A pretty blush tinted Jessica's cheeks pink, but she shook her head. "No, thanks, you've done enough. Besides, Freddie and I are going to have a quiet weekend. Other than his soccer game tomorrow morning we're just going to hang around at home. Sound good, bud?" she asked, ruffling the boy's hair.

"Can we play video games?" Freddie asked.

"After we wrap all the presents, sure," Jessica replied, making the child grin.

"All right then we'll see you Monday," the man said, still grinning widely.

"Bye, Jessica," the little girl said.

"Bye, Claire. Adam," Jessica returned, but her gaze kept darting in his direction.

After Adam and Claire left, Donovan closed the distance between himself and the mother and son pair. Jessica had a kid. On top of a demanding job. No wonder she looked exhausted and said she didn't have time to date.

"Who're you?" Freddie asked, eyeing the bouquet suspiciously.

"Freddie, manners," Jessica chided. "This is Mr. Davidson. His mom is Mrs. Grayson who owns Eat Dessert First."

"Cool." Freddie's eyes lit up. "How come you and your mom have different names?"

The question made him chuckle. Seemed like the boy, who appeared to be about seven, was a confident kid, he liked that. "Because when my mom married my stepdad she took his last name," he explained. "But you can call me Donovan, no need to be so formal and go with Mr. Davidson."

"This is Freddie. My son," Jessica added with emphasis, like she was trying to explain without saying it out loud that they were a package deal. Like he didn't already get that. Of course they were. He'd been raised by a single mom, he would never expect Jessica to prioritize anything else over her child.

That didn't mean she wasn't important, too.

She was.

And he intended to make that she knew it.

Kneeling so he was eye to eye with the kid, he balanced the bouquet in one hand and held out his other to shake the boy's. "Nice to meet you, Freddie. Baking brownies with your mom sounds like lots of fun, I used to love baking with my mom when I was a kid."

"We always bake when Mom has time," Freddie said excitedly, missing the way his mother winced.

"You're a lucky guy," he said as he straightened, absolutely meaning it. The single parent life was rough, and yet from the looks of things, Jessica was handling it like a pro. "These are for you. Thought I'd deliver them in person from here on out."

Eyes widening, Jessica glanced down at her son before lifting her gaze to meet his again. "You're going to keep delivering flowers?"

If she thought he was backing off because she had a kid she was sorely mistaken.

No way was he backing off now. He wanted kids. Okay, so he hadn't considered being a parent this way but it was no deterrent.

"Only way I'm going to stop, green eyes, is if you tell me to."

CHAPTER
Five

December 9th
   11:52 A.M.

"Do you have any intention of listening to a word I say today?"

Guiltily, Jessica looked up from her phone to see Adam looking at her from his desk across from hers. Her partner didn't look annoyed with her, in fact, he looked a combination of amused and pleased.

Ever since Donovan had turned up at the precinct a few days ago, Adam had been as interested in the handsome billionaire as her son had been. Both men in her life had peppered her with questions, and while she'd done her best to be as vague as possible because she honestly didn't know what she was going to do about it all, she couldn't deny it was exciting.

Having a man show genuine interest in her, even knowing she had a kid, was new for her. Donovan was being respectful, not pushing too hard, while making his intentions more than clear.

He wanted to take her on a date.

Her.

A single mom who worked long hours as a cop.

Him.

A billionaire who looked like a model who almost definitely had women falling at his feet.

So why wasn't she?

Because this all felt too good to be true.

One burned twice shy.

While she liked to pretend that her ex dumping her the way he had, just walking away like everything they'd shared meant nothing, hadn't affected her, it had. It had messed with her self-confidence. Claiming she was too busy to date, while undoubtably true, was also a good excuse to not have to put herself out there. If Donovan wasn't being so persistent, she wouldn't have given him asking her out that first day a second thought.

Okay, maybe a second thought or two but nothing would have come of it.

"I've been listening to you," she told Adam. Which was pretty much a lie. While she wasn't ignoring him or anything, her attention kept getting captured by her phone.

Since Friday afternoon when Donovan had come by right when she was about to leave with Freddie things had changed. Even though she'd had his number from the first bouquet she hadn't used it because she'd been so sure that he would lose interest as soon as he learned she was a mom.

Only that hadn't happened, and after tucking Freddie into bed that night, she'd caved.

Ever since, they'd been exchanging texts and it made her feel so young and desirable, something she hadn't felt since she'd been made a single mom at twenty-two.

"You've been obsessed with your phone," Adam corrected with a chuckle. "Are you going to go for it with Donovan?"

It helped that her partner was so supportive. Although she had other friends, most involved in law enforcement, he was definitely her closest. They spent most of their time together, and before Adam and Jasmine got together, they'd helped each other out with the kids. Even now Adam still helped her with Freddie, she was just relying more on sitters these days to respect his new relationship.

"Yeah, are you?" a voice asked from behind her, and she swallowed what would have been a most unbecoming given her job and the toughness it implied squeak.

"Donovan," she said, turning to see him standing there. In his hands he had his customary bouquet. Since she'd had the weekend off, this morning she'd been surprised to find that he hadn't skipped either day, two bouquets sat on her desk waiting for her. Along with them had been a Lego set for each day, and she saw another in his hand now.

He was including her son.

While she wouldn't admit it to anyone, this morning when she'd seen the Lego boxes sitting alongside the flowers she'd actually teared up. Freddie had good people in his life, role models, people she knew he loved and trusted, who cared for him, but he didn't have his dad. Her ex hadn't just walked away from her but their child as well and she hated that now her son had to suffer for the choices of someone who should have always put him first.

"I took a guess on the Lego. I knew my brothers and I loved them when we were Freddie's age. If he doesn't like them just tell me what he does like," Donovan said.

In the few days he'd known she had a son he'd shown more care for Freddie than her ex had in the last five years. "He *loves* Lego. He's going to be very excited tonight to see that you got him some gifts, but, Donovan, you don't have to get him anything. Me either. It's not necessary."

"Course it's not. That's why they're gifts," Donovan said, brushing off her concerns.

But they *were* concerns.

It wasn't like she was poor, she was able to pay her rent and bills, put food on the table, treat her son every now and again, but Donovan was a billionaire. He could afford anything he wanted, and she didn't know him well enough to gauge if he was the kind of man who threw money at things and used it to get what he wanted.

She and her son weren't a prize to be bought.

"So, are you going to give me a chance?" Donovan asked a tiny flicker of doubt in his gray eyes.

"I have a son, I have to put him first."

"Wouldn't expect or ask you to do anything differently. Is Freddie's father in the picture?"

"No."

"Do you want him to be?"

Jessica couldn't help making a face at that. "For me? No way. He walked away from us. For Freddie? Yeah, I wish his dad cared enough about him to be a father. But I've accepted reality, and if you're really trying to ask me if I want to get back together with my ex then the answer is absolutely not. Those feelings died a long time ago."

The smile Donovan gave her made her toes curl and her stomach flutter. "Happy to hear that, green eyes. So, what's stopping you from letting me take you out on a date?"

That was an easy question to answer, and a simple one.

Fear.

Fear of getting her heart broken, fear of Freddie getting his broken, fear of rejection, fear of not being enough for a man like Donovan Davidson.

CHAPTER
Six

December 10th
   4:49 P.M.

This wasn't really stalking, but for some reason, it felt like he was close to the line.

Donovan reminded himself that he wasn't. Jessica hadn't said no, she hadn't asked him to stop sending flowers, and she'd been the one to reach out via text.

Yesterday, when he'd dropped off flowers and Lego to the precinct and he'd asked her if she was going to give him a chance he hadn't gotten a no or a yes as an answer. She'd told him she needed time to think about it, to talk about it with her son, and he respected that.

So this definitely wasn't stalking.

Could he help it if the dossier he'd had his security people do on her had also included her address?

Feeling a little guilty as he watched Jessica's car pull into the driveway of the little house where she lived with her son, he shoved those feelings aside. As interested as he was in Jessica, he also had to be careful. He was rich and some people would try to take advantage of that.

Plus, he currently had a stalker. Just because they were all fairly certain who it was didn't mean he should stop being cautious. And just because he had no reason to believe Jessica would in any way be involved it also didn't mean he should throw caution to the wind.

Besides, he was going to confess to the dossier.

Donovan grabbed the large white box from where he'd buckled it into the passenger seat and headed across the street. Jessica and Freddie were chattering away and didn't see him until he was halfway up the driveway.

"What are you doing here?" Jessica asked, sounding surprised but not angry. Although, that anger could still come when he told her his people had looked into her and done a thorough background check.

"Donovan!" Freddie said, sounding a lot more enthusiastic than his mom. "Thanks for the Lego, they were so cool. I already put one of them together last night after I did my homework."

"You're welcome, buddy, I'm glad you liked them."

"I love them," the little boy corrected. "I asked Santa for a whole bunch of Lego for Christmas."

He made a mental note to ask Jessica later if she'd been able to buy them all, and if not, he'd get whatever she hadn't.

"We weren't expecting you to pop around," Jessica said. "I wasn't aware you even knew where we live."

"Yeah, about that," he said sheepishly. "My people did a background check. Nothing personal, green eyes, I swear. I just have a situation that requires me to be extra careful at the moment."

"A situation?"

"A former employee who didn't take kindly to being let go even though it was more than warranted and we worked with them every step of the way to try to resolve the issues. I have people handling it, but it doesn't hurt to be too careful," Donovan explained, hoping she could understand this had nothing to do with thinking she was anything other than what she was—a hardworking, dedicated mother and cop—and everything to do with how interested in her he was.

"Do you need help with this?" she asked, compassion and concern in her pretty green eyes.

"I have it under control." The last thing he was going to do was add another burden to the plate she already had piled high with responsibilities.

"What's in the box?" Freddie asked, eyeing it with interest.

"I'm glad you asked."

"You know you don't have to bring us things every day. The house already looks like a florist opened up shop there with all the flowers," Jessica teased.

"Ah, but this is something special," he said, holding the box out, low enough that Freddie could see inside, and opened it with a flourish.

"Dessert!" Freddie squealed in excitement. "Lots and lots and lots of desserts."

"Are those from your mom's restaurant?" Jessica asked with a hungry expression, eyeing the cakes, pastries, chocolates, fudges, and brownies he'd asked his mom to make.

"Yep. I told her I've been trying to woo you and thought the chocolate would work in my favor."

Red stained Jessica's cheeks. "You told her you've been sending me flowers? I don't think your mom likes me after the way we met."

"Nonsense. She was happy to know the local police department was there to protect her restaurant, she just got a little mama bear in the moment." Absolutely true. When he'd told his mom he was interested in Jessica her eyes had lit up with delighted glee. Only his little sister was still in her twenties, and she'd join him and their two older brothers in their thirties next year, and so far, they were all single. His mom wanted grandkids, and even the hint of a serious relationship was enough to get her excited.

"What's woo?" Freddie asked.

Unsure of how Jessica wanted to answer that particular question and not wanting to overstep, Donovan looked to her.

"Woo is a grown-up word that means a man wants to go on a date with a woman," Jessica said in a tone that made the whole thing sound boring.

It worked.

Freddie shrugged. "Oh." His gaze moved back to the dessert. "Mom, I'm hungry."

"Dinner first before you feast on all this sugar," Jessica told her son in a mom voice he recognized from his childhood. It was the tone that meant business, and Freddie knew it too because he shouldered his backpack and headed for the front door.

Watching her son, Jessica fiddled with the keys in her hand, clearly nervous.

Donovan kind of liked knowing she was nervous, too, at least he wasn't the only one.

This whole wooing thing was hard, and he hadn't even gotten on the field yet.

"Umm, did you want to come in and ..." Jessica paused, blew out a breath. "Have some dessert with us?"

Score.

Relief hit Donovan hard.

Finally, he was starting to make some progress, taking that first step onto the field.

"I'd love to, but I'm not sure you're ready for that yet. I want to take you out, green eyes, want to get to know you, and your son. But I want you to want it as badly as I do."

Mindful of the fact that little eyes were watching, Donovan leaned down and touched a kiss to her forehead before turning and walking back to his car. Walking away was hard, but it was the right move.

For now.

But as soon as Jessica was willing to give him a chance, he was jumping all in.

CHAPTER
Seven

December 11th
7:03 A.M.

"Mom, are you really going to let Donovan woo you?"

The question, asked so innocently by her seven-year-old son, caught Jessica completely off-guard.

Last night, she'd been expecting Freddie to ask about Donovan, about the flowers, the Lego, the box full of more desserts than either of them could eat, even though she'd given them both a small dinner so they could fill up on sweet treats. But last night he hadn't been interested in talking about anything other than his day at school, some YouTube video he and his friends were all nutty over, and the soccer game next weekend where they were taking on a team they'd never beaten and had determined this would be the first.

Now it seemed he was ready to ask about their future.

Jessica was painfully aware that whatever choice she made she wasn't just impacting her own life but her son's as well.

That made knowing what she was supposed to do that much harder.

If it was only her heart on the line, then maybe—*maybe*—she would be able to take that risk, but getting her little boy hurt would scare her off men for the rest of her life.

Grabbing both their plates, she sat down at the kitchen table opposite her son, she needed to be able to gauge his reactions to this conversation. Just because Freddie was a mature kid who hardly ever caused her much trouble didn't mean she wanted to parade a man into his life without knowing there was going to be a happy ending.

Only there was no way for her to know how things would work out if she gave Donovan a chance.

Maybe she'd fall in love and have the perfect family life she'd always dreamed of, but maybe she wouldn't.

Once already she'd given into those dreams and gotten burned.

Trying it a second time was so much harder.

"Honestly, Freddie, I don't know," she told her son.

"You don't like him?"

"I don't know him well enough to decide whether or not I like him." That was both true and untrue. There was attraction there, and so far, Donovan had been insistent but not in a pushy way, and respectful of her.

Those things had also been true of her ex.

They'd been high school sweethearts. With both their parents urging, they'd gotten married the summer before starting college. At the time she'd felt so grown up, so sure that she was going to spend the rest of her life with him that it hadn't mattered that she'd been pregnant at nineteen and a mom at twenty. She'd thought she had a partner who would always be there for her.

After all, those were the vows they'd made.

For better or worse.

Only life as a young parent, all the responsibilities of work, home life, and raising a child, had been too much and he'd bailed.

"He buys you flowers," Freddie pointed out.

"Buying things for people doesn't make someone a good person." Just because she liked the flowers, and just because she liked the fluttery feeling in her stomach every time a new bouquet arrived, Jessica was trying to approach this with more logic than emotion.

"He bought me Lego," Freddie added. "And he bought us dessert. I like him."

"You do?" Kids often were a good judge of character so even though he was seven she took Freddie's feelings seriously.

"Yeah. And if he woos you, maybe we can eat at Mrs. Grayson's restaurant for free," Freddie gushed, making her chuckle at the simple way a seven-year-old approached life.

"We wouldn't want to take advantage."

"It's not taking advantage if they're family." Freddie paused, his face growing serious. "If Donovan woos you, are we going to become a family? Is he going to be your husband? Is he going to be my new dad?"

Since she hadn't dated after the divorce, they'd never had to have this kind of conversation. But Jessica knew there were other kids with single parents at his school, and some of those parents had dated or remarried, so it wasn't like her son wasn't aware of what grown-ups did.

"Well, it would depend," she said slowly. "No, we wouldn't be a family right away, but yes, maybe someday we would be. Sometimes when adults date, it doesn't work out, and if it does then oftentimes, they do get married. If we did that would make Donovan your stepdad. But I don't know how things will work out, Freddie. Nobody does. There's always a risk when you let someone woo you. But I want you to know one thing for certain. No matter what happens, I will always be there for you. If I dated Donovan and we broke up, it would still be me and you against the world. And if I dated him and it worked out, you would always be my precious baby boy. No matter if I had a husband, or even if one day down the line we had more children. My love for you is never conditional on who else is in our life."

Instead of the emotional response from her son she had been expecting, Freddie rolled his eyes and took a huge bite of toast. "I know that, Mom," he said so matter of fact that it made her laugh.

"Good, I'm glad you know how much I love you." Reaching over, she ruffled his dark locks making him scowl and bat her hand away. If there was one thing she knew for certain she'd done right with her son it was making sure he knew he was loved. That was a huge parenting win as far as she was concerned.

"I think you should let Donovan woo you," Freddie announced.

"You do?" It wasn't like she needed her seven-year-old's permission, but it certainly helped to have him on board.

"Course. Then you won't be so lonely."

"I'm not lonely, Freddie. I have you."

"Yeah, but you don't have a grown-up to love you."

Her son's simple words touched her deeply. How could her child see that she'd been lonely when she hadn't been able to recognize it?

The upside to keeping so busy was that she rarely had time to think about the relationships in her life that were missing. Apparently, Freddie had given it some thought, though.

Taking the risk and letting Donovan in without any guarantees was scary, but when she broke it down she had to look at it one way. Would she wind up regretting not giving him a chance?

CHAPTER
Eight

December 13th
6:58 P.M.

For some reason, it felt like he'd been waiting a lifetime for this moment.

Luckily, Donovan was a go-with-the-flow kind of guy because if he wasn't, he'd be wondering why he was so obsessed with a woman he'd only known for almost two weeks. As it was, he was willing to just go with it, the scorching attraction was just begging to grow into something more, and tonight was his chance to show Jessica that they could build something amazing.

He was sure they could.

Fairytales came true every single day, he'd witnessed enough of them firsthand to know. Sometimes, that fairytale wasn't falling in love. Sometimes, it was being given a safe home to live in, or a year's supply of groceries, or a job where you could be independent and support yourself. Starting his charity had been one of the best decisions he'd ever made, and now as he walked up the short path toward the bright red front door, he couldn't help but wonder if he was about to make another.

Right on time, he knocked on Jessica's front door ready to take her out on the first of what he hoped would be many dates. Tonight had to be special, though, because Jessica was special. She wasn't just some woman looking to get him into bed because he was rich, hell, she'd known who he was from day one, and it had taken her almost two weeks just to agree to give him a chance.

"No messing this up," he murmured aloud, a split second before the door was opened and his mouth fell open in shock.

So far, he'd only seen cop Jessica. At work she wore simple black pants, a blouse, and a sweater, with her hair pulled back in a ponytail, or twisted into a bun.

Tonight, she had physically and metaphorically let her hair down.

Hanging in soft waves around her face, she'd gone simple with the makeup but the sexy red lipstick made it almost impossible not to lean down and kiss her. Dark blue jeans molded to her toned legs, just like the green sweater—that perfectly matched her gorgeous eyes—molded to her chest, showing off her perky set of breasts.

She was stunning.

Stepped off the page of a magazine stunning.

"You didn't say where we were going. Is this okay to wear?" Jessica asked nervously, and only then did he realize he'd been staring at her without saying anything.

"You look perfect," he assured her. He'd given where he was going to take her tonight serious thought. There was his mom's restaurant, but he didn't want his mother hovering over them all night. There was a fancy restaurant but that wasn't really his style. He'd been ten when his mom married his stepdad. He hadn't grown up in the land of the rich and was not a fan of any place he had to wear a suit, or worse, a tux. So, he'd settled on a little Mexican restaurant his family used to go to the occasional time they ate out for a birthday treat when he was young.

"Good," she said, relief evident in her tone. "I wasn't sure if you expected a formal dress."

"Nope, I'm not really that guy unless I have to be." If it were any other woman, he probably would have taken her to the fancy restaurant, but he wanted Jessica to know the real him, not just the wealthy investment banker most people saw him as. "These are for you."

"More flowers," she said with a smile as she took the bouquet.

"Gotta keep up my streak," he said with a wink.

After she'd set the bouquet on a small table by the door, she followed him out into the cool night and down to his car. Of course, he held the door open for her, his mother would never let him hear the end of it if he didn't use his manners, then once they were both settled, he started driving.

"So, it's been a *really* long time since I did the whole get to know you thing," Jessica told him, fidgeting nervously.

"Red," he said immediately. "My favorite color."

"Actually, mine's also red," she said. "Fudge. Favorite food."

"Ooh, that's a tough one given how good my mom is at cooking. If I had to pick just one, I'd have to go with her homemade tacos. Fall."

"Winter. I know, I know, everyone always hates winter," she added when he made a face. "But I love the snow. Even when we're still getting it in April."

For the rest of the drive, they went back and forth, sharing their favorite TV shows, books, music, vacation destinations, and sports. By the time they reached the restaurant, Donovan knew more about her than any other woman he'd ever taken out for a meal combined.

They'd meant nothing to him, but fate was telling him this woman could wind up meaning everything to him. He'd talked through this all with his family, his brothers thought he was crazy being willing to just jump all in, but his mom and sister—romantics that they were—got it. Even his stepfather had been encouraging.

"Mexican food?" Jessica asked when they pulled into the parking lot, sounding a little surprised.

"My favorite. Actually, this restaurant holds a lot of special memories for me. After my sperm donor left—I call him that because I don't even remember him and he left my mom with an infant, a one-year-old, a two-year-old, and a three-year-old to raise alone—things were tight. Really tight. We lived in a two-bedroom apartment, my mom and us four kids, we got all our clothes second-hand from thrift stores. More times than I'm sure I realize, my mom went hungry so us kids could eat something. She made sure we knew we were loved, she was firm but loving, and we all helped however we could. No matter how tough times were, every single birthday, Mom would bring us here for a special treat. I used to love those nights, and I thought I'd share this place with you."

The smile she shone on him told him he'd made the right choice.

Life could change in an instant, he'd learned that as a kid, going from poverty to luxury almost overnight. That had taught him to live in the moment, to not give voice to all the worries and what ifs, which was how he was able to jump all in with this woman regardless of the fact that they'd just met, and he had no idea what the future held for them.

CHAPTER
Nine

December 13th
10:46 P.M.

All night Jessica had been debating what she would do in this moment.

There was the smart option, which was simply to thank Donovan for a wonderful evening, for good conversation and great company, and maybe give him a goodnight kiss on her doorstep before saying goodbye and beginning the game of waiting for him to call.

He was going to.

That she knew with absolute certainty.

But still she would wonder and wait, anxiety would take hold, and she would over analyze every single thing she'd said and done, looking for anything that might have turned him off even after he'd been patiently persistent for almost two weeks while she got herself ready to say yes to a date.

That was for sure the smart option.

There was another, though.

One that wouldn't get out of her mind every single time he shot her one of those charming smiles, or his finger brushed against her hand or arm. Every time heat flared in his eyes, or she looked over to find his appreciative gaze lingering on her breasts or her backside.

Why was this even a debate?

She knew exactly how she wanted this night to end, she just wasn't sure she was brave enough to do it.

"When is too soon to call?" Donovan asked as his hand captured hers as they walked toward her front door. "Tomorrow morning first thing before the sun gets up? As soon as I get back to my mom's house? When I get in the car?"

The last one made her chuckle and relieved her anxiety. Just because she'd been out of the dating game a long time and had only ever been out with one man anyway, it seemed she hadn't managed to turn him off.

Drawing in a deep breath, she steadied her nerves and decided to just go for it.

What was the worst that could happen?

If she jumped in too deep and got her heart broken, she'd find a way to mend it. Find a way to mend her son's as well. But not going for it when Donovan had been everything she could hope for in a man and then more, would teach her son that you gave into your fears and let them control you.

The last thing she wanted to do was curb her little boy's natural curiosity and inquisitiveness. She wanted him to live his life to the fullest, reach for his dreams and find a way to succeed at them no matter what they were.

"How about you don't call," she suggested, rushing on when Donovan's face fell. "How about you don't call because you come in and spend the night."

Desire, hot enough to scorch her skin with a single glance was quickly replaced by a look of concern. "Jessica, I hope you know I would never pressure you for sex. I know this was a big step for you and you have a son to consider. I can wait as long as it takes for you to be ready."

"So, you don't want to come inside?" she asked, taking a step closer until there was practically no space between their bodies, and cupped the bulge in his pants.

"Oh, beautiful, nothing would make me happier, but I'm not going to be the kind of guy who pressures a woman."

Which was exactly why she was comfortable with him coming in.

"You're not pressuring me," she assured him. "I want this. Want you."

With a groan he reached out, hands spanning her hips, and lifted her. "I want you almost more than I can breathe," he whispered, lips against her ear, then trailing a line of kisses down the column of her neck.

"Mmm," she moaned, tilting her head to the side to give him better access. Those soft kisses were little touches of aphrodisiacs, and if she hadn't already been burning for him that definitely would have set her desire alight.

"Keys," Donovan demanded, and she fumbled in her bag and handed them over.

Once they were inside, his mouth claimed hers in a searing kiss that felt almost like a brand. It was the craziest thing, after getting her heart broken, she would have sworn that she could never hand it out again. Yet Donovan made it so easy to do.

He was a genuinely likeable guy and already he had her hooked.

All that was left was for him to reel her in and she'd be a goner.

Without directions, he located her bedroom on the left side of the big open-plan living space, and when he set her on her feet a mewed protest tumbled from her lips making him chuckle.

"Got to get these clothes off you, green eyes," he told her, nuzzling at her neck as his hands found the hem of her sweater and pulled back only long enough to remove it and toss it aside. Then his lips were back, touching kisses to her pebbled nipples before removing her bra and kissing his way down her stomach until he was kneeling in front of her.

Her pants seemed to almost remove themselves, and when his dark head moved so it was buried in the apex of her thighs, she almost came on the spot.

Never had she seen anything sexier.

"So sweet," he murmured, making her protest again when he suddenly stood and stripped off his own clothes.

Then he had her in his arms again, carrying her to the bed, laying her out, then stretching out his body above her. His thick length nestled between her legs, and she quickly spread them, anxious to feel him inside her.

Even though he'd barely touched her, it had been so long, and her body was already rushing toward the inevitable conclusion.

"So sweet," he said again as he kissed her long and slow, then moved so he could slide on the condom he'd grabbed from his pocket.

His fingers touched her, tracing lazily around her entrance before sweeping up to circle her bud. Each touch wound her higher and higher until she knew she was balancing on the ledge, ready to tumble into indescribable pleasure.

"Donovan, inside me, please. I want you to come with me."

The smile he gave her was tender as he shifted and then thrust inside her in a single move. It had been so long that there was a moment of pain as she was stretched, but Donovan's slow, steady thrusts quickly erased it, and then she was back on that ledge.

"You ready, beautiful?" he asked as his gaze locked on hers.

"Feel like I've been waiting forever for this moment," she answered.

"Me too, green eyes. Me too."

With that, his mouth crashed down against hers, and one of his hands reached between them and tweaked her bundle of nerves, setting off the most explosive orgasm Jessica had ever experienced in her life.

It consumed every single inch of her body, mind, and soul, and with it, Donovan Davidson took the first step inside her closely guarded heart.

CHAPTER
Ten

December 14th
   2:27 P.M.

A smile hadn't left his face all morning.

Donovan felt like he was floating on cloud nine.

The most perfect first date ever had ended with more than he had expected. Given her reticence to just going out on a date with him, there was no way he would have expected Jessica to be okay with sex.

Yet she was.

More than that, she'd seemed to need it.

It had been amazing, not that he had expected anything different, but more importantly it seemed to have solidified a spot for him in her life.

Since Freddie was having a sleepover at her partner Adam's house, she'd asked him if he would like to spend the night with her. There was only one answer to that question, and he'd proved that with a kiss before settling between her legs and making her come all over again.

That had been followed by a round of shower sex before they both climbed into her bed. Long after sleep claimed her, he'd laid awake simply watching her. He had no idea what it was exactly about this woman that had him so obsessed, but he was consumed by her. Wanted to learn every single thing there was to know about her and forge bonds not just with her but with her son as well.

Love at first sight.

There was no other way to describe it.

His soul had just recognized her.

This morning, Jessica was a lot more relaxed around him and they'd talked more while he cooked her breakfast. They'd spent the morning together, and he'd only headed out when it was time for her to go and pick up her son.

As much as he'd love to just pick them both up and move them into his place so he could see them every day, he understood and respected why Jessica had to move more cautiously. While he knew for certain that she felt the same magnetic pull as he did, she had a child to consider.

So, he would play things the same way his stepfather had when he started dating Donovan's mom. From the very beginning, the man he now called dad had made it clear that he was interested not just in their mom but in them as well. He'd spent time with them one-on-one, taken them out on "dates" without their mom as well as family "dates" where they could all get to know one another. It wasn't just that he'd bought them lots of stuff, although as kids they had loved the gifts, it was that he made them feel important and valued, something their biological dad never had.

That's what he wanted to do with Jessica and Freddie. Show them that he could be there for them both, that they would never have to worry about whether or not he was trustworthy. He'd fight any dragon that tried to hurt them no matter what it was.

Which was why he was still grinning as he sat in his office.

Although it was Saturday, he'd been taking more time off lately. Between Jessica and Freddie, and the stalker who managed to remain undetected despite reaching out to him numerous times, he'd fallen behind on a few things. Since he employed only the best of the best, he wasn't worried about it affecting business. His employees could and had been picking up the slack, but he was still the boss, and he needed to spend a few hours today checking in and making sure everything continued to run smoothly.

Just as he typed in his password, his phone dinged with an incoming text.

His smile grew wider as he reached for his cell, expecting the text to be from Jessica.

That smile slid off his face when he saw the text.

You don't get to date

A cold shiver rocketed through him.

The stalker knew he'd been out with Jessica last night.

The police had been involved in this mess from almost the beginning, since as soon as he realized it wasn't just someone wanting to mess with him a little but someone who could become a legitimate threat. The texts had progressed to his car being vandalized, and blood filled balloons being thrown at him while he was entering and exiting the building. Then it was attempted break ins at his penthouse, and threatening letters being delivered to his office.

Pretty quickly the cops had settled on a suspect. A former employee who had been caught filtering money out of clients' accounts and into his own. Instead of owning up to it, the man had doubled down, insisted he was being framed, and thrown a huge fit when he was fired. According to the cops, after losing his job the man had then lost his wife who had committed suicide when their lavish lifestyle was ripped away from them when the stolen money was reclaimed.

Hard as he knew the cops were working on locating the man, he'd seemingly disappeared off the face of the Earth. He used a new disposable cell every time he texted, they had no idea where he was living, or how he was supporting himself since he wasn't accessing bank accounts.

Yet he was hanging around close enough that he knew Donovan was now dating a woman. Had he watched them last night? Did he know where Jessica lived? What would he wind up doing to her if Donovan kept dating her?

Those were questions he didn't want to know the answers to.

What was he supposed to do now?

Did he break up with Jessica, destroy the threads of trust they were building, in an effort to keep her safe and out of his stalker's firing line?

Could he do that?

Could he just walk away from her, knowing that even when the stalker was caught, he might not get a second chance with her?

Jessica's heart was still healing from her ex's betrayal, and he was all too aware that in these early stages, all it would take was one wrong move and he'd lose her for good.

But at least she'd be alive.

Fear over what his stalker could do left him almost paralyzed.

It felt like he was in a no-win situation, and whatever choice he wound up making he could lose everything.

CHAPTER
Eleven

December 16th
   7:13 A.M.

"Mom, I can't find the Lego that Donovan gave me," Freddie complained as he strolled into the kitchen.

"What?" Jessica asked, distracted. The high she'd been riding Saturday afternoon when she kissed Donovan goodbye and went to pick up her son had slowly faded until she was sitting right in the middle of the pit of anxiety she had been so worried about when he brought her home from their date.

Something was wrong.

Something had changed.

There was a distance between them that hadn't been there before, and she couldn't stop analyzing what she'd done to cause it.

It all started when she texted him around dinner time on Saturday. He'd replied, but there had been a delay. Not that she expected him to be sitting around just waiting to hear from her, but she usually got a reply text within ten or fifteen minutes, this time it took almost three hours.

Maybe he'd been busy with work.

Maybe he'd been out with his family.

Both logical answers.

Yet the one that stuck in her mind and refused to budge was the maybe he'd only been interested in sex and the good guy act was just a way to lull her into a false sense of security so she would give it up. Now that she had, there was no need for him to hang around.

That didn't feel right, but she had to remind herself it was only just over two weeks since she'd met the man. How could she really know him well enough to judge?

One delayed response wouldn't have her this worked up, but all day yesterday, when Donovan did answer texts, they were always short and abrupt. She could feel him distancing himself and it hurt and made her angry.

At him.

At herself.

At life in general.

"Mom," Freddie whined. "I said my Lego are missing. The new ones. They're gone."

"They can't be gone," she told him, setting a plate of toast on the table and indicating he should sit and eat so they weren't late to school and work.

"They are," he insisted.

"They probably just got mixed up with all your others. You have like four boxes full of the stuff."

"No, they can't have. They were still in their boxes. I hadn't built them yet."

"I'm sure they're around here somewhere."

Before Freddie could argue the point, the doorbell rang, and she hurried to open it. When she did she saw the last person she expected standing there.

"Donovan," she greeted him, resisting the urge to throw herself into his arms. Just because he was there now didn't eliminate the feeling that he was backing away. There was no bouquet in his hands, and his expression was troubled.

Something was definitely up, and she could guess what it was.

"Can I come in? We need to talk."

"No." Instinctively, she moved to block him, pulling the door mostly closed behind her as she stepped onto the porch. Her son was in there and if Donovan was breaking up with her she didn't want him to hear it. So far, Freddie wasn't invested in this relationship, so he wasn't going to get hurt. On the other hand, she was and would.

"I understand." His hand rubbed at the back of his neck like it was stiff, then dragged down his face. "I'm sorry for being a little distant over the weekend."

Jessica didn't offer him any acceptance.

It wasn't okay to play with her feelings.

"It's not what you're thinking. It's not that I got sex and lost interest, or that anything changed. Well, it did change, it made me crave you more, but that's not why I was distant. When I got to my office after leaving here on Saturday I got a text from my stalker. They told me that I didn't get to date."

Over dinner Friday night he'd told her about his stalker, so she knew about the former employee who had been stealing money, denied it, then wound up losing his wife as well as his job. It would make sense that the stalker wasn't keen on the idea of Donovan dating when his own wife had taken her life.

"I'm scared," Donovan admitted. "Not for me, but for you. You and Freddie. I don't want to pull you into this mess, and you wind up getting hurt. I've spent all weekend debating whether I should just end things with you so you'll be safe, or trust the cops to keep you safe."

Now that she knew his reasons for putting distance between them she could relax. Jessica got his position, it sucked, he wanted to make the right one for everyone but didn't know what it was. Offering him a smile she reached out and took his hand. "Have you forgotten I *am* a cop. Thank you for worrying about me and my son, but I can look out for us. Now that I know there could be a threat, I can take extra precautions, but I don't want you to walk away, Donovan."

"You don't?" He seemed genuinely surprised by her decision.

"No. Of course not. A relationship is supposed to be two people together working on solutions to problems, not one person trying to handle things on their own. I've been there and done that, and I have no intention of going through it again. I want a partner who will work with me, not against me."

Wrapping an arm around her waist, he tugged her up against him. The tension she'd felt emanating from him when she opened her door had melted away and the smile she was used to seeing on his face was back. "How did I get so lucky that a woman like you would take a chance on a guy like me?"

"We'll get this issue sorted, I'll help however I can. We're not going to let your stalker steal our chance at happiness, because I feel pretty lucky, too," she admitted, resting her cheek against Donovan's chest and soaking up the feel of his arms wrapped around her.

She'd pushed aside her fears and taken a chance on a man even though her history urged her to play it safe. There was no way she was letting some criminal stalker take away a man who was quickly coming to mean a lot to her.

No way.

CHAPTER
Twelve

December 17th
6:03 P.M.

"Did you know that I got to meet Santa one time when no one else was here?" Freddie babbled excitedly from the backseat.

"You did? For real?" Donovan asked, managing to keep a straight face when all he wanted to do was chuckle. He hadn't spent a whole lot of time around kids. None of his siblings were in a relationship, none had kids, and his only friends who had kids employed nannies who did ninety percent of the work so he never really saw them. While he'd worried a little at first that Freddie wouldn't warm to him, or he wouldn't know how to talk to the kid, it seemed like he shouldn't have worried.

Jessica had done a great job raising her son. He was confident and polite, open and engaging, curious and excitable, full of energy, and had a lightness to his soul that told Donovan that Jessica had shielded him emotionally from the fallout of his dad leaving and having no part of his life.

"For real," Freddie assured him. "Claire's new mom owns this whole place, and one day when I was staying at Adam's house we got to come here, and Santa was taking a break, and I got to talk to him. I mean, he's not the real Santa, you know?"

"He's not?"

"No, course not. The real Santa is too busy to come and work here and meet all the kids, so he trains special Santas to do that for him. They listen to the kids tell them what they want for Christmas and then they go to the North Pole and tell the real Santa. So even though he wasn't the real Santa he works for him."

"That's definitely cool," Donovan agreed, loving the way the Christmas Farm had set things up in a way to keep the magic for kids alive. He'd never been to this place before, although, of course, he'd heard about it, and he was as excited as Freddie to visit tonight.

Although she'd been a little reticent about this school night excursion, Jessica had given in prettily easily when he told her that he wanted to spend time together with the three of them. While he didn't expect her to just allow him to step right into the role of dad, he also knew that since Freddie's dad was not in the picture, he would eventually be filling a role that had been left empty, and he wanted to do a good job of it.

"Super cool," Freddie corrected, practically bouncing in his seat as Donovan managed to find them a parking spot in the almost full lot. With just over a week before Christmas, the place was packed with happy families, and he relished the opportunity to be one of them.

"What do you want to do first?" he asked once they'd all climbed out of the car and rugged up in coats, scarves, beanies, and gloves.

"Snowmen then reindeer," Freddie announced before his mom could get a word in.

Unsure if they were following along with the kid's plans or if Jessica was in charge, he glanced at her as he took her hand, and they headed for the front gate.

She shrugged. "Unless there's something you really want to do it's fine with me to do what Freddie wants."

"I've never been before, so I think we can let the expert take charge."

"You've never been here before?" Freddie sounded aghast at the thought.

"Never had a kid to come with."

"Well, now you got me." Freddie slipped his hand into Donovan's free one and he swore right there and then the kid just barreled his way right into Donovan's heart.

"Now I've got you," he echoed. Simple words yet they meant a lot to him. This mother and son duo was already carving out a special place in his heart and life, and the more time he spent with them, the more attached he was getting.

It was busy but the line moved quickly, and a short while later they'd bought tickets, walked through the gates, and were heading to a huge open field that had been dubbed Snowman Land. There were squealing kids everywhere, and lots of laughing, smiling moms and dads soaking up the joy on their kids' faces.

This was definitely something he could get used to.

Already he'd had fun choosing Christmas gifts for both Freddie and Jessica, and he was hoping he could persuade them to spend a little time on Christmas Day with him, although he was yet to broach the topic.

Snowman Land was huge, and there were stalls everywhere around the perimeter with all sorts of costumes and props you could use to dress your snowman. There was everything from the traditional coal for eyes and mouth, carrot for the nose, and scarf for his neck, to way more complex ideas. There were superheroes and princesses, animals in a range of species, and firefighters and ballet dancers. Donovan couldn't wait to see what Freddie would choose to dress up his snowman as.

"Basically, you just make your own snowman, then choose your outfits and put them on. Then you can take pictures, but there's also a photographer here if you want something more professional, although you have to pay for those ones," Jessica explained as Freddie went running to an empty part of the field, dug his hands right into the snow, and began rolling it into a snowball.

"We'll definitely get the professional ones," he told her.

"Freddie will be happy enough with whatever we take on our phones," Jessica protested.

"I'm sure he will, we're still getting the professional ones."

"You don't have to spoil him."

"Oh, beautiful." Donovan stopped and tugged Jessica closer, his arm around her waist keeping her anchored against him. "I'm going to spoil him. I'm going to spoil you both. I think it's past time somebody did and I'm just glad that somebody gets to be me."

After dropping a kiss to her lips, he hurried after Freddie, leaving her standing behind him staring at him. If she thought he wasn't going to spoil both her and her son rotten then she was crazy. These two were his now, he'd protect them, he'd take care of them, and he'd spoil them, because he wanted them to be happy and know they were cared about.

If the stalker thought he could be blackmailed into walking away from them he was crazy, these two were already a part of him and no one was going to mess with them.

CHAPTER

Thirteen

December 17th
7:36 P.M.

They came here every year.

Every single year from Freddie's first Christmas onwards.

After Adam and Jasmine got together last Christmas, they'd even been several times throughout the year. While the place was obviously the busiest at Christmastime, it operated all year long, and they'd enjoyed riding horses in the spring, playing in the fields in the summer, and picking fruit in the autumn, and all the other activities the place offered.

But this visit was her favorite.

Watching Freddie and Donovan bond was such a special experience, and Jessica was so glad that she'd decided not to let her fears get the best of her and had given Donovan a chance. It was clear her son already liked and respected him, and it wasn't just because Donovan bought him whatever he asked for.

Already they'd had gingerbread, cotton candy, popcorn, candy canes, fudge, and chocolate, hot chocolate, and warm apple cider.

They'd had professional photos taken with their snowman and the rein-deer when they'd moved on to the next encounter. They'd even taken a reindeer pulled sleigh ride. Sitting in the sleigh, covered with blankets, with Freddie snuggled between them, Donovan's arm around her shoulders, she'd felt so happy she was sure she was going to burst.

Now they were in the snowball ring, and she'd already given up on getting Freddie home at a reasonable hour, which had been the one condition she'd had when she agreed to this impromptu family date.

Who cared if he was tired tomorrow?

It was almost Christmas break, and her son deserved to have some fun and be spoiled. He was such a good kid, he never complained when she couldn't afford to buy him something the other kids had. He was respectful to her and never got angry about the fact that he didn't have a dad even though she regularly cursed her ex—in her head never to her son's face—for abandoning such a great kid just so he could live his own life without responsibility.

Staying on the sidelines to give Donovan some time alone to bond with Freddie, she giggled as she watched the two throwing snowballs at one another as quickly as they could make them. While Donovan didn't outright let Freddie win, he put up a fight, made sure a couple of his snowballs hit the excited child, he was also careful to make sure that even more of Freddie's snowballs hit him.

She already knew he had what it took to step into the role of father. Not that she thought it would be a perfect ride, she was sure there would be bumps along the way, nothing in life went completely smoothly, but she also knew that if things kept going well between them he wouldn't just make a good husband but a good dad, too.

When her attention was caught by a little girl looking scared and alone, she straightened and hurried over. Freddie was fine with Donovan for now, but this little girl looked like she had lost sight of her parents.

Being both a cop and a mom, she noticed when most of the other people around her were too caught up in their own families, and when she reached the child, she knelt so they were eye to eye.

"You lost, sweetie?" she asked.

"I can't see my mommy," the girl, who looked to be about four told her, tears brimming in her big blue eyes.

"My name is Jessica, and I'm a police officer, I'm sure I can help you find your mom. What's your name?"

"Lissy."

"That's a pretty name. Was it just the two of you here together, Lissy?"

"No, my daddy is here, too, and my brothers. They was fighting with the snows balls, and they weren't listening like they were 'posed to. I was following mommy and daddy when they chased after my brothers, but there were too many snows balls and I got scared, then I looked and they were gone," the girl explained.

"I'm sure they're here somewhere, sweetie. Which direction were they going?"

"That way." Lissy pointed down toward the back of the field where it joined the woods surrounding the farm.

"Okay, let's go take a look. We don't want you missing out on all the fun, do we?" she asked, standing and taking the little girl's hand.

"I wanted to throw snows balls too," Lissy told her as they both started walking.

"I bet you did. Are your brothers bigger or smaller than you?"

"Both. Chase is bigger than me, but I'm bigger than Gary. They fights together alls the time."

"Brothers can be like that." Not that she would know firsthand, she didn't have any siblings, but Adam was almost like a brother to her and even though he drove her crazy sometimes she couldn't imagine a better partner or friend, and knew she was lucky to have him in her life.

They reached the trees, and Jessica gave the area a visual sweep. She didn't want to go traipsing through the woods because they were huge, and it was easy to get lost in there. They'd take a quick look, and then if they didn't see Lissy's family, she'd take the girl back to the entrance to the snowball park and have her wait there while she organized people to look for her family.

Movement just a little way into the trees caught her attention and she relaxed, sure it was the girl's family. Knowing they'd probably realized by now that Lissy was no longer following them they must have been worried and torn. Chase after the boys or look for their daughter, they might have even split up so they could do both.

"Hello? I have Lissy here with me, she got lost," Jessica called out as she took a step closer to the movement she'd spotted.

Too late she realized she'd made a mistake.

She'd let her guard down. She wasn't on duty tonight, she was just here as a mom and girlfriend having family fun.

Something slammed into the side of her head and the world around her vanished.

CHAPTER
Fourteen

December 17th

7:44 P.M.

It wasn't until he heard the screams that he realized something was wrong.

Donovan had been so engrossed in his game of snowballs with Freddie that he hadn't been thinking of anything else.

They were at a crowded theme park, what could possibly happen?

Wasn't like the stalker was going to walk through a crowd of happy families and attack him or Jessica and Freddie.

Would he?

Terror clawed at his insides as he instinctively reached for Freddie and pulled the little boy close. The same thing most parents seemed to be doing as the shrill scream sounded again.

"Where's my mom?" Freddie asked, looking over to where Jessica had been just moments ago.

Now the spot was empty.

"Lissy?" a woman shouted out, and he could see a couple with two small boys running toward a little girl who was the one doing the screaming.

Because Jessica was gone, he picked up Freddie and followed the couple. Something was wrong, and it had to do with this little girl, he knew it.

"Don't you *ever* wander off again, you hear me?" the woman was saying as he approached. She'd dragged the sobbing little girl into her arms and was trying her best to calm the distraught child.

"The police lady gotted hurt," Lissy was babbling through her tears.

Police lady?

Jessica?

"Sorry to interrupt," he said, approaching cautiously, not wanting to upset the family but needing to know what was going on. Obviously assuming it was nothing more than a child who'd temporarily gotten lost most other people had resumed their playing, but Donovan couldn't shake the feeling there was more to it than that and the little girl's words confirmed it.

"Yes?" the father said, moving to stand between him and his family.

"My girlfriend is missing, she's a police officer," he explained.

"The police lady fell down," the little girl said again.

"May I?" he asked the parents, stepping closer when they nodded. "You're Lissy?"

"Yeah."

"I'm Donovan, and this is Freddie. Did you get lost?"

"There were too many snows balls, and I couldn't see Mommy. Then the police lady was there, and she said she'd help me. But when we went looking, someone hit her, and she fell down," Lissy told him.

"Was the police lady's name Jessica?" he asked, already knowing the answer.

"Yes," the child whispered.

"Please call the cops," he said to the family as he debated leaving Freddie with them while he went looking for Jessica. As much as he didn't want the child out of his sight, he also didn't want him to see his mother hurt, or possibly worse.

It was the worse that had him in a near panic.

The stalker's threat echoed in his mind.

"I'll go with you, I'm a doctor," the father said. "Your boy can stay with my wife while we go check on his mom."

"I want to stay with you," Freddie said, his thin arms tightening their grip around Donovan's neck until it was almost strangling him.

"I want you to stay with me, too, buddy, but I think your mom would prefer you wait here with Lissy and her mom. I'll come right back to you as soon as we make sure your mom is okay. All right?"

Freddie sniffed but nodded, and he set the little boy down, then leaned in to give him one more hug.

With the other man on his heels, he took off toward the tree line where the little girl had come running from. What was he going to find when he got there? Had Jessica just been injured or was she dead or dying right this very second?

As soon as he got close enough, he spotted the bright blue coat she'd been wearing.

It was lying in the snow, unmoving, and the closer he got, he could see that the snow around her head was stained red.

How had he ever thought the color was his favorite?

Now red would forever remind him of this moment, of the woman he was falling for lying motionless in the snow, blood oozing out from a head wound.

Dropping to his knees beside her, he barely felt the cold from the snow seeping into his jeans. He had to know.

Dead or alive.

Had he already lost her before he'd even really had a chance to be with her?

Had his interest in a woman cost a little boy his mother, the only parent he had?

Ripping off his gloves, he touched his fingers to her neck and sagged in relief when he felt it.

A pulse.

Alive.

Not gone.

"She's got a pulse," Donovan told the other man.

"Looks like she was hit over the head with this." The doctor pointed to a branch lying discarded by Jessica's side, then knelt beside her and began to examine the wound. As he probed it Jessica groaned, her eyelashes fluttering against her pale cheeks.

"Jessica? Can you hear me, sweetheart? It's Donovan." Carefully as he could, he brushed his knuckles across her cheek, terrified of doing anything to hurt her.

She mumbled something incoherent.

"Jess?" He tried again. "Answer me, baby."

"Freddie?"

"He's okay," he assured her.

"The little girl ... Lissy ...?"

"Is okay, too. It's you we're worried about right now."

"Head hurts," she mumbled, still fighting to open her eyes.

"It's going to be okay, ma'am," the doctor told her. "An ambulance is coming, we'll get you to the hospital. Likely concussion, possible hypothermia," the doctor said to him.

All things considered, Donovan knew they were lucky and knew things could have been a lot worse. If the stalker was out for blood, a girlfriend for a wife, then he could be looking down at her dead body right now. Whether this was all the stalker had intended to do, or if Lissy's screams had deterred him from doing more, Donovan would never know, and it terrified him.

This time they'd been lucky, but what about next time?

CHAPTER
Fifteen

December 18th
   12:18 A.M.

Her head throbbed, and all she wanted to do was sleep for about a million years.

Everything was too bright, too loud. Even though the hospital room had the lights turned down low, it still hurt her eyes. The only sound was the soft snores of her son as he slept curled up on Donovan's lap, but even that was enough to aggravate the pounding behind her eyes.

Not that she wanted the sound to stop.

It reassured her that her son was okay, alive and safe, mostly untraumatized by the events of the evening.

Jessica would be forever grateful that he hadn't been with her when she'd been attacked.

"You should be sleeping," Donovan told her, voice soft and low so as not to wake the sleeping boy, but she was sure also so he didn't make her headache worse.

"Can't. I feel ..." She couldn't even put into words exactly what all the emotions tumbling around inside her were. Fear for sure, anxiety, uncertainty, embarrassment, shame. She was a cop and yet she hadn't paid attention to her surroundings, hadn't let the seriousness of the situation with Donovan's stalker keep her alert, and had paid the price for it.

A price that was much lower than it could have been.

Instead of sitting in a hospital bed with a concussion and some mild hypothermia from lying out in the snow, she could have been seriously injured or even killed.

The stalker had lost his wife, so it made sense that he might want to take any woman Donovan had in his life.

"I'm so sorry," Donovan told her. The guilt in the gray eyes looking back at her made the nausea swirling in her stomach so much worse. He was not responsible for the choices his stalker made. He was every bit as much a victim as she was, more because he was the target and had been for months now.

"Not your fault." When she wiggled her fingers against the mattress he reached out and grabbed them, clinging tightly.

"Of course it is."

"We don't know for sure that it was your stalker who attacked me. Could have been anyone."

Donovan scoffed. "Yeah, you just happened to get knocked unconscious by a random weirdo at a family theme park at the same time that I have a stalker who threatened you."

"It's a possibility," she told him. Just because she agreed with the timing and there was a good chance it was his stalker, didn't make it so. There very well could have been a "random weirdo" watching the happy families and waiting for a chance to make a move. Besides, it wasn't like Donovan's stalker could have known she was going to walk away from the crowd and right toward where they were hiding if they were following Donovan around.

"Not a very likely one," Donovan muttered. "I'll understand."

"Understand what?" Between the headache and tiredness, she had no energy left to figure anything out. If he wanted to say something he was going to have to be clearer than that.

"If you want to break things off with me."

"Why would I want to do that?"

"Because you almost definitely were attacked tonight because of me. Because someone wants to blame me for stealing money from my company and my clients, and then getting caught. For the fallout from having all their assets seized and their wife deciding she'd rather end her own life than deal with it all. This is my fault." The hand holding hers moved to sweep across the bandage taped to her temple. "And I wouldn't blame you if you don't want to put yourself or your son in danger because of me."

Reaching up, Jessica reclaimed her grip on Donovan's hand. "I'm not blaming you for someone else's actions. I don't want to leave you," she assured him. She would however be taking better precautions from here on out. Especially since the concussion would put her at a disadvantage for at least the next couple of weeks.

"You don't?"

"Course not. Don't be silly," she said with a yawn.

"I'm always going to feel responsible for this." Donovan's fingers tightened around hers, and she could feel the guilt and fear rolling off him in waves.

"I don't want you to."

"Can't help it, green eyes." He gave her a one-sided smile, and then his face grew serious. "At least let me take care of you while you're healing. You have a concussion, you shouldn't be going home alone, especially when you have a seven-year-old to care for."

"You want to come stay with us?" The idea actually made her smile instead of filling her with panic that she couldn't have a man staying in her house, not this soon in their relationship, not when they were still in the getting to know one another phase, it was too soon.

None of that was how she felt, though.

All she felt was a pleasant sort of warm and fuzzy feeling at the thought of him wanting to take care of her. Even when they'd been married and she'd been sick, heck, even when she was pregnant with their child, her ex had never been one to want to look after her.

Caring for others was her job. She was the woman. He was the big, strong, tough man whose sole purpose was just to bring in the money.

"Actually, I was thinking you and Freddie could come and stay with me at my mom and stepdad's place. I've been staying there since the stalker started targeting my penthouse. They live on a beautiful estate, there's good security, you'll be safe there and you won't have to worry about anything but getting better, I'll take care of everything else."

Stay with Donovan?

At his parents' house?

Despite him saying otherwise, she still believed his mom didn't like her.

Wasn't staying with him going to give Freddie the wrong idea?

Only was it really a wrong idea?

Sure, they were in the early stages of their relationship, but she wouldn't have let a man meet her son if she wasn't serious about him, and every indication he'd given said Donovan was just as serious about her.

About them.

Both of them.

Because he was taking good care of her son right now.

Hoping it wasn't the concussion leading her to make bad decisions, Jessica prayed this was not going to be something she wound up regretting.

"Okay, we'll stay with you while I'm healing."

CHAPTER
Sixteen

December 18th
4:32 P.M.

Even with the guilt he felt about Jessica getting hurt, Donovan couldn't help smiling as he parked outside his parents' house and rounded the car to get Jessica.

Freddie bounced out, his wide, excited eyes taking in the grand mansion. "Wow, this house is huge," he gushed.

"I think I might have forgotten to mention it has a pool," Donovan told the little boy then opened the back door and reached in to scoop Jessica into his arms before she could try to climb out herself.

Finally, after agreeing to stay with him while she recovered, she'd managed to get a few hours of sleep, and she'd been discharged a couple of hours ago. After a brief stop at her place to pack bags for her and Freddie, he'd driven them both here. She was nervous about staying here, he got that, but he loved that she was trusting herself with him while she was vulnerable.

"A pool!" Freddie squealed in excitement. "Can I go swimming now?"

"Sure can. The pool is indoors so you can use it all year round, even when it's snowing outside," he said, glancing at the sky and the mass of gray clouds that looked like they could start dropping snowflakes at any second.

"You have to ask Donovan's mom first," Jessica told her son.

"She won't mind you swimming," he assured Freddie as he carried Jessica up the front steps. "She's very excited you're both staying here for a while. She's been getting rooms ready for you both, and I think she's been busy in the kitchen, too."

"Did she make some of her brownies?" Freddie asked.

"Pretty sure that was top of the list."

"Yay," Freddie exclaimed just as the front door was thrown open and his mom and dad came rushing out.

"Oh, you poor thing," his mom said, beelining directly for Jessica. "I'm so sorry you were hurt, but I'm so thrilled for a chance to get to meet you properly."

"I'm sorry about how we met first," Jessica said, shrinking into his arms a little.

"Nonsense. You were just doing your job." His mom waved a hand in the air, dismissing the entire thing. "And who is this handsome young man?"

"My son. Freddie."

"I hear you like brownies, Freddie. I have a fresh batch cooling in the kitchen."

"Can we have some while they're still hot?" Freddie asked, bouncing about excitedly. "Mom always lets me have one while they're still all warm and gooey."

"Of course we can."

"Mom said I had to ask if it's okay if I go swimming after," Freddie said in a tone that suggested the notion was a little silly, but he was going to indulge his mother anyway. "Donovan said you have a pool. One that's inside so we can go swimming all the time."

"Brownies and swimming, sounds like a fun afternoon," his mom said, beaming at the child. "Then if you like, you can help me cook some dinner."

"Oh, no, you don't have to entertain him. He brought books, and

Lego, and some video games, he'll be quiet and keep out of your hair," Jessica said.

"Nonsense," his mom said again. "It's been far too long since I've had a youngster to spend time with. I'm looking forward to getting to know young Freddie here, so you just rest and recover, dear, and don't worry about a thing. Your boy is in good hands."

While his mom ushered Freddie inside, with his stepdad following, an amused smile on his face, Donovan carried Jessica inside. "Do you want to have some brownies or go right up to bed first?" he asked.

Eyeing the hall his mom and her son had disappeared down, he could see in her face Jessica was having an internal debate. He knew it wasn't that she didn't trust his family to look after her son, it was that she wasn't used to having a support system like this. She had her partner, and he knew they'd helped each other out over the years, but she didn't have family, so this was new to her.

"I think I might take a nap first," she finally said, resting her head against his shoulder and making his heart swell in his chest.

Not only was she there, safe and sound, snuggled in his arms, trusting him to take care of her, but she was trusting him and his family to take care of her child as well and that meant everything to him.

Carrying her upstairs, Donovan headed for the room his mom had prepared for her. It was right next to his, and the room beside that was where Freddie would be staying since he knew Jessica would want her son close by.

"This your room?" she asked on a yawn as he carried her into it and over toward the four-poster bed.

"I would have loved to have you in my bed, but no, my mom and I thought you might not be comfortable with that since Freddie is here too," he told her as he balanced her in his arms and pulled back the covers.

"Thank you." She caught his hand as he set her down and went to grab the blankets to tuck her in. "For inviting me to stay here, for wanting to take care of me. Not just me, but Freddie, too. For making him feel so welcome here."

"You are both welcome here," he told her, sitting on the edge of the bed and palming her cheek. "Whatever happens between us you will always have a home and a family here. I hope one day we'll fall in love, get married, and add more kids to our family. But even if that doesn't happen my family will always be there to support you and Freddie."

"That's sweet," Jessica said, her eyes fluttering closed. "I hope we get our happy ever after though."

"Me too, beautiful," he whispered as she drifted off to sleep. Leaning down he pressed a kiss to her forehead. As much as he wanted a happy ever after with this woman and her son, there was a pretty big obstacle standing in their way.

His stalker.

CHAPTER
Seventeen

December 20th
5:23 P.M.

Another Friday night, another date.

Only this one was a whole family affair.

More than that, it was inviting Donovan into a special tradition that she and her son shared.

Every Christmas they bought a bunch of little, cheap gifts, wrapped them up in the traditional bright and garish Christmas wrapping paper, and dropped them off on their neighbors' doorsteps. Freddie always had so much fun doing it, and even though it meant losing a little bit of the budget she would have spent on gifts for her son, Jessica had always felt that the trade-off of him learning about giving was well worth it. Besides, she always managed to get him the things he wanted the most and he was young enough to not even know that he could have gotten a couple of extra toys if they didn't do this.

Better to give than receive.

That was an important motto, and she wanted her son to learn it. Wanted him to know that helping others and doing nice things for them without expecting anything in return, was the way to make the world a better place. She was pretty darn proud of her son for already knowing that when so many adults didn't. The joy and excitement he got each year when he got to put on his Santa hat and play at being the jolly gift giver reassured her that she was doing this whole parenting thing pretty alright.

"Are you sure you're up to this?" Donovan whispered in her ear as he helped her into the car. He'd been so sweet these last couple of days, fussing around her like a mother hen, making sure she was okay, ensuring she took her pain pills on time, and ensuring she ate even if it was just a little soup. He helped her shower and get dressed, carrying her around so she didn't have to walk. He took care of Freddie, made sure he was entertained, took him to school yesterday and today, and helped him with his homework.

Honestly, he'd been perfect. There was nothing more she could have asked of him.

"Positive," she assured him. Even if she wasn't there was no way she was going to miss out on this special Christmas tradition. She would drag herself out of her sick bed, which given the constant headache and lingering dizziness and nausea, she was actually doing just that because this was one of her favorite things to do in the festive season. Actually, it was something she looked forward to all year.

"All right then, let's get busy being Santa Claus," Donovan said, buckling her seatbelt for her then checking to make sure Freddie was buckled in before starting the car.

Christmas music played inside the vehicle as they sang and giggled on the way back to her and Freddie's neighborhood. Even with the threat of the stalker hanging over their heads, and her injuries, there was plenty of Christmas spirit to go around.

"Where do you want to start?" Donovan asked when they came to a stop outside her house. Usually, they dropped off little presents to all the houses with kids on their block. Nothing extravagant, some doll's clothing, a soccer ball, some nail polish, or matchbox cars, just a little something to let people know they were special and cared about.

"Mrs. Hunter's house," Freddie replied immediately. While the elderly woman didn't have any children, she also didn't have anyone in her life. Her husband had been gone for almost twenty years and she had no other living relatives. It always broke Jessica's heart that the poor woman spent Christmas alone, despite her many invitations to join her and Freddie, so she always made sure they included a gift for her as well.

"I think I'll wait in the car," she told the boys as they climbed out.

"Are you sure?" Donovan asked, sticking his head in the open car door. "I know this is your thing to do with your son. If you want, I can wait in the car or even at your place."

Smiling so he knew that this wasn't just because she wasn't feeling great after the head injury, she gave a small shake of her head. "You don't need to do that. I want you to be involved, and so does Freddie. I'm fine here, I can watch you two play Santa."

"Come on, Donovan," Freddie urged, fiddling with the fluffy pompom on the end of his Santa hat. "The street is quiet, no one will see us, but if we don't go now, we might get caught."

For a little boy, trying to drop off the gifts without getting caught added a whole new layer of fun and excitement.

"You got it, buddy."

Grabbing the first present from their bag in the trunk, Donovan took Freddie's hand, and she watched as the two of them looked up and down the street, then darted into the front yard of Mrs. Hunter's house. Like the funny, crazy goofballs that they were, they darted from tree to tree, then onto her porch. While Freddie carefully set the present on the mat, Donovan hung a candy cane from the doorknob.

Then they slunk back through the yard, giggling and whispering to one another as they went. By the time they scrambled back into the car both of their eyes were twinkling, their cheeks pink from the cold, she'd forgotten all about the pain in her head.

How could she think about it when there was so much joy flooding the car?

There was no way this time last year when she and Freddie had done this together, she could ever have predicted that in just a year's time there would be a man in their life. Even a week ago when she went out on her first date with Donovan and asked him to spend the night, she couldn't have predicted that she would have fallen this hard this fast.

But she had.

And she didn't regret a single thing.

Life was to be lived, and that's what she was finally doing. No more hiding, she was getting out there and taking her life by the horns.

No stalker who wanted to destroy her newfound happiness was going to win.

No one was taking this future away from her and her son.

CHAPTER
Eighteen

December 23rd
5:01 P.M.

Everything was perfect.

That's how Donovan felt as he shut down his computer and prepared to take the first proper vacation he'd had in years. Running a business the size of his required near-constant dedication. Long hours and sacrifices, those had all become the norm for him these last few years.

Not that he was complaining.

Donovan knew how lucky he was. That he'd had a mom who loved him, that she'd made the best life she could even when she didn't have a lot to work with. Their stepdad was such a great guy who didn't just love his mom but also loved him and his siblings. They'd never had to worry about money again after moving into their stepdad's home. He'd gone to good schools, an Ivy League college, been able to travel the world, and his father's connections had allowed him to build a successful business and become wealthy in his own right.

All of that meant a lot to him, but none of it compared to how Jessica and Freddie made him feel.

They filled him in a way that nothing else ever had. They gave him a purpose that made him feel like a well-rounded person. They completed him. Seeing their faces each morning was the perfect way to start the day, and he loved being the last thing they both saw at night before they went to sleep.

And the best thing was he had an entire lifetime to enjoy those little moments.

Now, he was heading home to spend the holidays with his girl and his little boy, and he couldn't be happier. Jessica was probably healed enough that she was okay to go back home, and they'd decided that she would after the holidays, but for the next two weeks they were going to stay in his penthouse. He'd tripled security, upgraded his system, and he was confident that his stalker wasn't going to be able to get to them there.

Their own little Christmas vacation. Just the three of them, in his penthouse, he'd made plans for several things they could do, both him and Jessica as a couple as well as family things. He couldn't wait.

The building was quiet as he walked through it. Tomorrow was Christmas Eve, and he'd decided everyone was to take the whole day off. They'd had a Christmas lunch today, he'd handed out bonuses, and everyone else was home already.

Vacation time had begun, and as much as he was looking forward to a quiet staycation, he was also planning all the places he wanted to take Jessica and Freddie. There were so many amazing countries in the world, so many spectacular cities, he couldn't wait to open that up to them. That was one of the things he'd loved the most as a kid, the toys, nice house, and new clothes were all great, but nothing compared to taking your seat on a plane ready to travel the globe.

That was a feeling he wanted to share with the people he already considered his own little family.

When his phone buzzed, he pulled it out, expecting the text to be from Jessica. She and Freddie were decorating the penthouse today. He'd dropped them off on his way into his office this morning, and he'd already received at least three dozen pictures of Christmas trees and tinsel, garlands and decorations. Every time he replied with a warning for Jessica not to overdo things.

A warning she didn't seem to be taking seriously.

As much as he was enjoying seeing the smiles on her and Freddie's faces, it had only been five days since she was knocked unconscious. She was still suffering the side effects of the concussion, and he was worried she was going to set herself back. That was the last thing he wanted with Christmas just two days away.

These memories would last them all a lifetime, and he wanted their first Christmas together to be a special one.

One look at the phone told him this was not another Christmassy photo.

It wasn't Jessica's name on his screen.

The message was from an unknown number.

Which of course meant he knew who it was from.

His stalker.

At least Jessica and Freddie were safe at his penthouse with an alarm, armed guards both down in the building's lobby and at the top of the lift outside the front door to his home. No way could his stalker get to them.

They were safe.

Safe.

The reassurances did little to calm his racing heart as he read the text.

I warned you and you didn't listen

The cops had told him not to engage with the stalker, that it would only be giving them what they wanted. They wanted his fear, they wanted his attention, they wanted to know they were getting to him, that they were affecting his life.

But this time he wasn't sitting back and being passive.

He'd had enough of this, he wanted it finished, wanted to end this now and move forward with his life.

> Leave them alone

> They have nothing to do with this

> I told you not to date her

> What happens next is on you

There was something in the tone of the message—odd though that sounded since they were just words on the screen—that had the hairs on the back of his neck standing up.

> Turn yourself in

> Sooner or later you're getting caught

> Don't make this harder on yourself

> You're the one making it harder on yourself

> You should have listened

> This is all your fault

> Where are you?

Standing outside your front door.

The bottom dropped out of his world.

If the stalker had made it to his door, that meant the guards he had watching over Jessica and Freddie had somehow been neutralized, leaving his family alone and unprotected with him on the other side of town and no way to get to them in time.

CHAPTER
Nineteen

December 23rd
5:10 P.M.

A knock at the door caught her by surprise.

Jessica glanced at her watch. It was after five, and Donovan should be on his way home by now, but there was no way he could be there already. Even if he was, there was no reason for him to knock on his own front door, this was his place after all not hers.

Although she did love the pretty penthouse.

It had gorgeous views across the city, a huge living room that she could already picture the three of them sitting in together, playing board games or building with Lego. The kitchen was also huge with enough space for a large table even though there was also a formal dining room. There was another cozier living space, more of a den, which looked like the perfect spot to curl up on a cold winter's night, turn on the TV, and binge-watch a show. There were four bedrooms, all of a generous size, and like everything else in the penthouse, the master was also huge with the biggest bathroom she'd ever seen in her life. It was kind of a shame she'd opted for one of the guest rooms since she would have loved to share it with Donovan, but she didn't want to rush things when she had a child to consider.

Staying with him was only for while she recovered. After the winter break, when Freddie went back to school the two of them would be moving back to their place. Of course, she'd keep dating Donovan, and when they both felt like the time was right for all three of them they'd get married and move in together.

But not yet.

Definitely too soon.

A second more impatient knock at the door had her giving the newly decorated room a final glance before heading for the foyer. It was likely one of the guards Donovan had hired to watch over them all while they stayed there. There were supposed to be two downstairs and one standing outside the lift so no one could get up.

Still to be safe, Jessica brought up the camera feed to check. Before he left this morning Donovan had set up her phone so she had access to all the security cameras. Just as a precaution, they'd both believed she was safe there.

Jessica still believed she was.

On the screen was Donovan's secretary.

Worry took hold inside her. Had something happened to Donovan? There should be no reason for the secretary to be there unless there was something wrong. What that could mean, though, she had no idea. Had Donovan been in an accident? A problem at his building? Sick? Hurt? Had there been another issue with the stalker?

"Mom, who's at the door?" Freddie asked, wandering out of the kitchen with some crackers. Her son was certainly making himself at home. He'd loved staying with Donovan's parents, loved that they'd fallen quickly into the roles of doting grandparents, and he loved that the building the penthouse was in also had a pool.

Her little water baby was a sucker for any body of water he could go swimming in. Pool, lake, ocean, it didn't matter to Freddie, as long as he was swimming he was happy.

"It's Donovan's secretary," she told him as she unlocked the door and opened it.

As soon as she did, her cop instincts sprang to life.

Something felt wrong.

Although the woman who was about her age was smiling and had a stack of brightly colored Christmas boxes in her arms, Jessica had been a cop long enough to know that trusting her instincts could be the difference between life and death.

If something felt wrong then it was.

"Jana, Merry Christmas," she said, forcing a smile and acting nonchalant while also trying to move slightly so she blocked entry to the door. Her son was inside and while she had no logical reason to view this woman as a threat, she was going to treat her as such until she proved otherwise.

"Merry Christmas," the woman returned, crowding forward.

Standing firm, Jessica looked over her shoulder, her gaze searching for the guard who should be out there.

When she couldn't see him her anxiety amped up.

"May I come in?" Jana asked.

"Actually, we're waiting on Donovan. I'm surprised you didn't come with him." Keeping her voice polite, she also made it clear that she knew something was up. The stalker was an ex-employee, that was what Donovan had always believed, what the cops believed, but what if they were wrong?

She'd looked through the evidence. There was nothing concrete—no security footage, no fingerprints, no DNA—to prove the identity of the stalker.

Was it possible that it was actually Donovan's secretary?

"I won't take long. I just want to drop off these gifts. Donovan asked me to," Jana added as though that was going to make a difference.

Only it wasn't.

Whatever was going on, she wasn't going to try to figure it out now while her seven-year-old son was there. She was certainly going to be bringing it up with Donovan and the cops working on his case as soon as he got home, though.

"I'll take them in," she said, holding out her hands.

Taking a step back, Jana's smile faltered for a moment before she righted it. "Actually, Donovan said there shouldn't be any peeking," she said with a fake-sounding chuckle.

"We have dinner on the stove," Jessica lied, moments away from just stepping back and closing the door. Maybe she'd even call the cops now, let them sort the whole thing out. The fact that she still couldn't see the guard was worrying her. Even if he thought Jana was a safe person to let up, he should still be there.

"Mom?" Freddie called out from somewhere behind her.

A split second too late Jessica realized her mistake.

At the sound of her son's voice, she automatically turned her head toward him.

That was all Jana needed to take advantage.

The next thing she knew she heard the familiar sound of a gun cocking.

CHAPTER
Twenty

December 23rd
5:19 P.M.

It felt like a lifetime since he'd gotten the text message threatening Jessica.

In reality, it hadn't even been twenty minutes.

Somehow, Donovan had managed to make it across town and to his building. The cops had ordered him to stand down, let them handle things, but he had no intention of sitting out there and waiting.

Not when Jessica and Freddie were upstairs.

There were no guards he could see in the building lobby and that told him everything he needed to know.

His stalker was there.

In his building.

Possibly already up in the penthouse.

As he ran toward the lift, it felt like he was trapped in a dream, one of those ones where no matter how hard you tried to move your feet seemed like they were encased in concrete. It took too long to reach the lift. Too long to punch in the code to get to the penthouse. Too long for the lift to go up past all those floors.

When the doors finally did open and he was standing in the lobby too many things struck him all at once.

The door to his home was standing open.

Scattered in the doorway was a pile of gift boxes.

Shoved off to the side was the still body of one of the guards.

Running quickly toward the body, a quick check of the guard's pulse told him the man was still alive. There were no injuries he could detect, and he assumed the man's attacker had drugged him.

Donovan shoved to his feet and ran inside his home.

It was quiet in there.

Deadly silent.

As he ran from room to room, finding them all empty, his fear continued to grow.

Where were they?

What had happened?

How had a stalker everyone was on the lookout for managed to not just get into the building but all the way up to his penthouse, and get the drop on an armed guard?

It didn't make sense.

He was missing something.

Only it was hard to think of anything other than his fear for Jessica and Freddie.

The sight of her phone lying discarded on the floor by the door caught his attention and he bent and scooped it up. She'd told him her passcode, and when he typed it in the phone immediately opened to a view of the security camera.

Could finding answers be that simple?

When he looked through the recent history his mouth dropped open when he saw who had knocked on his door this evening.

"No," he murmured aloud.

It couldn't be.

How could he have gotten things so wrong?

As he watched he saw his secretary, Jana, approaching the guard. Not suspecting her to be a threat he wasn't prepared for her to jab a needle in his neck. Once the guard had passed out, Jana knocked on his door and had an exchange with Jessica before producing a weapon and marching both Jessica and Freddie into the lift, which then headed up to the roof.

The smart move would be to stay there, wait for the cops, share what he'd learned, tell them where he believed they were, and let them handle it.

But that meant waiting.

And he couldn't do that.

So smart move or not, Donovan headed for the stairs that led to the rooftop garden. They were slightly off to the side so when he got up there Jana might not realize, and he could assess the situation and figure out how to get Jessica and Freddie out of there alive.

Still in shock that the person trying to ruin his life was none other than his secretary, he started up the staircase. Why would Jana do this?

They'd flirted when she first took the job a year ago. There had even been a night where he'd gotten uncharacteristically drunk and taken her to bed. In the morning he'd told her it couldn't happen again, he was her boss and they'd made a mistake. He'd thought Jana had taken it well, she'd told him she wasn't after more and then the whole mess had started with finding out someone was stealing from him, and to be honest, he'd never given her a second thought. She did her job and didn't make waves when she absolutely could have over his inappropriate boss behavior.

Now he knew she had been the one stalking him and she'd taken from him the two most important things in his life.

As soon as he reached the roof he spotted them.

Jana was trying to herd Jessica and Freddie toward the roof's edge. The building was twenty-five stories. If her intention was to push them over, then neither of them was going to survive.

Donovan knew he couldn't let that happen.

"Jana, why don't we just let Freddie go back inside. He has nothing to do with this and he's only seven," Jessica was saying as he slowly approached. She had her son tucked behind her, her body a human shield, and he knew she would do whatever it took to protect her child.

"No. The kid goes, too. Has to. You're both in the way," Jana mumbled, a manic tone to her voice he'd never noticed before.

"I'm the one in the way," Jessica countered. "He's just a little boy."

"No, no, no. It's both of you. He bought the boy gifts. I took them back, but it didn't fix anything. It wasn't supposed to be this way. He was supposed to be me. I knew he was mine from the moment I met him. I tried to show him, but he said it was a mistake. Then you came along. You weren't supposed to get in the way. When his life was falling apart, he was supposed to come to me," Jana snapped.

How much of everything that had happened was on her shoulders?

Had it been her all along?

Was she the one responsible for him getting drunk—on what at the time had been only two glasses of wine as far as he knew—the night they slept together? Was she the one who had been stealing? Who had set everything up? And for what? A chance to be with him? There had never been a chance of him turning to her for any reason, he just didn't feel anything for her.

"Go, climb over and jump," Jana ordered.

Even from where he stood, he could see the stubborn look on Jessica's face. She wasn't going to do it. She was going to try something.

With terror coursing through his veins that she'd get herself killed in an effort to protect her son, Donovan didn't think twice.

Just acted.

Lunging forward, he snapped a hand around Jana's wrist, shoving her arm up so the gun no longer pointed at Jessica and Freddie.

The woman startled, fought him, managed to break free of his hold, but she stumbled and lost her balance.

Fear filled Jana's eyes as her arms cartwheeled.

But it was already too late.

With a scream he'd never be able to get out of his head, she fell over the side of the roof.

They were standing there, frozen in place, until the scream was abruptly cut off.

Then Donovan reached for Jessica and Freddie, yanking them into his arms. He was never letting them go.

Not ever.

He'd had a taste of what it felt like to lose them and he didn't like it.

CHAPTER
Twenty-One

December 24th
   8:38 P.M.

"I can't believe he went to bed so easily," Jessica whispered as she carefully closed the door to Freddie's bedroom. "Last year he insisted he was going to stay up all night to catch Santa in the act. I let him lie on the lounge room couch and then carried him to bed once he fell asleep."

All things considered, Freddie was doing well in the face of yesterday's events.

Of course, she didn't think her son was going to escape from the ordeal unscathed, after all, he'd had a gun pointed at him and been told he was going to be killed. But she'd made an appointment with a child psychologist to make sure he could work through his feelings with a professional, as well as talking through it with him herself.

Last night, they'd come back to her house after giving the police their statements. Freddie had said yes when she'd offered to spend the night in his bed with him, and even though she'd told him he could go back to his parents', or sleep in her bed, or on the couch, Donovan had decided to sleep on the floor of her son's room.

Jessica was pretty sure the idea of letting either of them out of his sight terrified him.

She knew the feeling.

When Jana had had her and Freddie on the roof, ordering them to jump to make it look like a murder-suicide, she hadn't just been scared for her son and herself, but Donovan, too. When the dangerous woman realized he was never going to love her, she would have wound up killing him, too.

"He's a great kid, the best," Donovan told her, pulling her into his arms.

They would still be spending the rest of Freddie's winter break together, it would just be at her place rather than his penthouse. She was looking forward to the next couple of weeks when she would have nothing to do or worry about but spending time with her son and boyfriend. Spending Christmas Day with anyone other than her son would be weird because the last five years it had just been the two of them, but she was excited to share the joy of tomorrow morning with Donovan, and then have lunch with his family. Already she liked his parents, and now she'd get to meet his siblings, too.

"He is the best," she agreed, resting her head on his chest. "You ready to go play Santa with me?"

"Can't wait."

Together they set about placing Freddie's gifts under the tree and in his stocking. They ate the cookies, making sure to leave plenty of crumbs behind to add to the aesthetic, and drank the milk. They snapped the carrots in half and gnawed on the ends while she got out some glitter and shrugged into her coat.

"What are the sparkles for?" Donovan asked.

"Magic left behind by the flying reindeer," she explained with a wink.

Outside, they sprinkled some glitter around the house, Donovan even threw some up into the plants and trees surrounding the house so it looked like it had all landed there as the reindeer flew over and landed on the roof.

Once they were back inside, Jessica found herself yawning. While there hadn't been time yet for her to process what had almost happened yesterday, her focus had been on her son and his needs, the mental strain was weighing on her.

"You ready for bed, beautiful?" Donovan asked, helping her out of her coat and locking up behind them.

"Mmhmm, but I'm not quite ready for sleep."

"Oh no? And what do you want to do before sleep?" Donovan stood behind her, his arms wrapped around her waist, drawing her against him as his lips touched a kiss to the sensitive spot behind her ear.

"I think you can use your imagination."

"Thankfully, I don't have to use my imagination, I have you here in my arms, mine to touch, to hold, to pleasure," Donovan murmured, touching more kisses to her neck.

"Yours," she agreed, wondering at how easy it had been to jump all in to this relationship when she'd been so sure she would never trust a man again.

It was all Donovan.

He made trusting him so easy.

Yesterday, he hadn't hesitated to run right toward danger for her and her son. If that didn't tell her everything she needed to know about him then nothing would.

Picking her up, Donovan carried her into her bedroom, then took his time stripping her clothes off her. Each brush of his fingertips against her skin had heat growing inside her. By the time they were both naked she felt like she was about to burst if he didn't hurry up and get himself inside her.

"You ready for me, green eyes?" he asked as he backed her up to the bed and lay her down.

"Ready," she answered breathily, greedily, ready to take everything he would give her.

"Perfect, because I'm dying to taste you, touch you," he murmured, his breath warm against her most sensitive flesh when he settled between her legs.

The first stroke of his tongue had her hips flying off the bed. A chuckle rumbled through him, vibrating around her bud when his lips closed around it and he began to swirl the tip of his tongue around it, making her moan as sensations built.

It didn't take long for those sensations to mount and then explode inside her in a rush of pleasure that stole her ability to think. Before it could return he was there, thrusting into her, his fingers working her bundle of nerves, sending her first orgasm spiraling into a second one as she came all over again in a wave that seemed to go on and on forever.

But amazing as it was, when Donovan settled above her, his large body carefully balanced over hers, pressed close enough for her to feel every inch of him but not crushed by his weight, it was so much better. This man had come barreling into her life out of nowhere, helping her learn to trust again. In his arms she felt cherished and protected, she could take care of herself and her son, but it was nice to have someone there on her side to have her back.

This was definitely the best Christmas ever.

CHAPTER
Twenty~Two

December 25th
  6:42 A.M.

This was how he wanted to wake up every morning from here on out.

With Jessica's warm body snuggled against his side, and her son sleeping in his room across the hall. When he had them close like this, Donovan knew they were okay, although how he was going to cope at the end of winter break when Freddie went back to school and Jessica went back to work, and he had to let them out of his sight he had no idea.

Thankfully, Freddie seemed to have slept through the night without issue, but Jessica had had nightmares. He'd woken a couple of times to her thrashing and whimpering in her sleep. Each time he'd pulled her close, wrapping his body around hers and protecting her the best way he could.

Waking her with soft words and gentle kisses, reassuring her each time that she and her son were safe, that he was there. Each time she would tell him she felt silly reacting the way she was given her job, and he'd remind her being a cop didn't prevent her from being terrified when her own child was in jeopardy. Eventually, she'd fall asleep again, and he'd doze, wanting to be prepared in case she needed him again.

Never would Jessica struggle alone again.

Not on his watch.

From here on out, she had a partner who would support her in any way she needed him to.

The sound of footsteps in the hall had Jessica stretching, blinking open sleepy eyes. "And so it begins," she mumbled with a grin.

Seconds later, the door to the bedroom was flung open. If Freddie was in any way worried about seeing him in his mom's bed the kid didn't show it. His face was animated, and he was bouncing about excitedly.

"Mom, Donovan, come on! Let's go see what Santa left," Freddie said, buzzing out of the room with as much energy as he'd entered it.

"If you want I can give you two some time alone," he offered as Jessica climbed out of bed and slipped on her robe. While he wanted to be involved in this morning's fun and festivities, he didn't want Jessica to feel like he was forcing his way into her and her son's lives before she was ready.

"I don't want, but thanks for offering." Standing on tiptoe, she brushed her lips across his and then took his hand, leading him down the hall and out into the large living room.

Freddie was already there, standing beside the plate with cookie crumbs and the mostly empty glass of milk. "Look, Santa ate the cookies we baked for him!"

"I'm sure he loved them, you're a good baker," Jessica told him, dropping a kiss to the top of the child's head before she dropped down onto the couch.

"I'm going to be even better because Sylvia is going to teach me to bake all the things she makes for her restaurant," Freddie gushed as he dropped down in front of the tree.

"My mom is a great teacher," he told Freddie as he handed the boy his Christmas stocking.

The next half an hour flew by. It had been a long time since he'd experienced the joy of Christmas morning from a child's point of view, not since he and his siblings were kids, and then it was only from a child's perspective. Now as an adult, sharing in the joy and laughter with Freddie as he opened each gift and gushed about his new toys, he realized how much his mom must have enjoyed these precious moments, and understood why she was angling for grandkids.

There was nothing like the pure joy and love filling this room.

By the time all the presents were opened, wrapping paper and empty gift boxes were everywhere. New Lego sets had made up most of Freddie's gifts, as well as some clothes, a few miscellaneous stocking stuffers, and the new skateboard he'd wanted. With Jessica's permission he'd given Freddie an iPad. While he would have loved to buy the boy a new one, Jessica had said it wasn't necessary so it was only an old one he had lying around, but it was loaded with apps, and the boy had been ecstatic about it.

"Mom, can I go ride my skateboard?" Freddie asked.

"Breakfast first. Then you can ride for a bit, but we have to leave at noon for lunch with Donovan's family. Why don't you get to work on one of those Lego sets while I give Donovan his gift," Jessica suggested.

"Can I give him my gift now?" Freddie asked, skateboard forgotten.

"Yep, sure can."

Scrambling under the tree, the little boy came back out with two wrapped packages in his hand. "We made these at school with our art teacher," he explained. "I always make something for my mom, but this year I made this for you, Donovan."

His heart swelled in his chest, and he couldn't wait to see what the boy had made for him, but Jessica went first. Always. "Mom, first," he said.

Carefully unwrapping the paper to reveal a glass jar decorated with hearts made out of little fingerprints, with a candle inside, Jessica beamed at her son and grabbed hold of him, pulling him into her arms and showering his face with kisses making him giggle and squiggle. "Thank you, baby boy, it's the most beautiful candle holder ever."

"I did the hearts all in red because that's your favorite color," Freddie told her.

"You know me well, my boy."

"Open your present now, Donovan," Freddie ordered.

When he took the gift it was heavier than he'd been expecting, and already from the shape of it he could figure out what it was, but he didn't say anything until he opened it. When he'd removed the paper, he saw that Freddie had painted pictures all around the handle of the hammer, and he beamed at the boy, loving the gift. "Thanks, Freddie boy, I love it."

"My mom's not so good at fixing stuff when it breaks," Freddie informed him. "But now you can help us fix stuff."

He absolutely would.

Not because Jessica needed him to fix her life for her, she'd been doing just fine on her own, working hard, and raising an amazing kid, but because he wanted to be there with her, sharing in the ups and downs of life.

"Christmas hug," he said, reaching for Jessica and Freddie and pulling them both into his arms. As excited as he was to give Jessica his gift—a gold locket with a heart made of rubies on the front and a picture of Freddie and his snowman inside from the night of their first family adventure—right now he just wanted to hold onto these two tightly, be grateful not just that they'd survived his stalker's attempts to kill them, but that they had both been so willing to give him a chance.

He was one lucky guy, and he wanted to make sure he never forgot it.

Will Christmas bring happiness to Donovan's sister Macy and the single dad who saves her life? Holiday Sorrow coming Christmas 2025

Holiday Sorrow (Christmas Romantic Suspense #9)

Also by Jane Blythe

Detective Parker Bell Series

A SECRET TO THE GRAVE
WINTER WONDERLAND
DEAD OR ALIVE
LITTLE GIRL LOST
FORGOTTEN

Count to Ten Series

ONE
TWO
THREE
FOUR
FIVE
SIX
BURNING SECRETS
SEVEN
EIGHT
NINE
TEN

Broken Gems Series

CRACKED SAPPHIRE

CRUSHED RUBY

FRACTURED DIAMOND

SHATTERED AMETHYST

SPLINTERED EMERALD

SALVAGING MARIGOLD

River's End Rescues Series

COCKY SAVIOR

SOME REGRETS ARE FOREVER

SOME FEARS CAN CONTROL YOU

SOME LIES WILL HAUNT YOU

SOME QUESTIONS HAVE NO ANSWERS

SOME TRUTH CAN BE DISTORTED

SOME TRUST CAN BE REBUILT

SOME MISTAKES ARE UNFORGIVABLE

Candella Sisters' Heroes Series

LITTLE DOLLS

LITTLE HEARTS

LITTLE BALLERINA

Storybook Murders Series

NURSERY RHYME KILLER

FAIRYTALE KILLER

FABLE KILLER

Saving SEALs Series

SAVING RYDER

SAVING ERIC

SAVING OWEN

SAVING LOGAN

SAVING GRAYSON

SAVING CHARLIE

Prey Security Series

PROTECTING EAGLE

PROTECTING RAVEN

PROTECTING FALCON

PROTECTING SPARROW

PROTECTING HAWK

PROTECTING DOVE

Prey Security: Alpha Team Series

DEADLY RISK

LETHAL RISK

EXTREME RISK

FATAL RISK

COVERT RISK

SAVAGE RISK

Prey Security: Artemis Team Series

IVORY'S FIGHT

PEARL'S FIGHT

LACEY'S FIGHT

OPAL'S FIGHT

Prey Security: Bravo Team Series

VICIOUS SCARS

RUTHLESS SCARS

BRUTAL SCARS

CRUEL SCARS

BURIED SCARS

WICKED SCARS

Prey Security: Athena Team Series

FIGHTING FOR SCARLETT

FIGHTING FOR LUCY

FIGHTING FOR CASSIDY

FIGHTING FOR ELLA

Prey Security: Charlie Team Series

DECEPTIVE LIES

Christmas Romantic Suspense Series

CHRISTMAS HOSTAGE

CHRISTMAS CAPTIVE

CHRISTMAS VICTIM

YULETIDE PROTECTOR

YULETIDE GUARD

YULETIDE HERO

HOLIDAY GRIEF

HOLIDAY LOSS

HOLIDAY SORROW

Conquering Fear Series (Co-written with Amanda Siegrist)

DROWNING IN YOU

OUT OF THE DARKNESS

CLOSING IN

About the Author

USA Today bestselling author Jane Blythe writes action-packed romantic suspense and military romance featuring protective heroes and heroines who are survivors. One of Jane's most popular series includes Prey Security, part of Susan Stoker's OPERATION ALPHA world! Writing in that world alongside authors such as Janie Crouch and Riley Edwards has been a blast, and she looks forward to bringing more books to this genre, both within and outside of Stoker's world. When Jane isn't binge-reading she's counting down to Christmas and adding to her 200+ teddy bear collection!

To connect and keep up to date please visit any of the following

www.ingramcontent.com/pod-product-compliance
Lightning Source LLC
Chambersburg PA
CBHW020730250626
47155CB00006B/2230